TWO SUPER HEROES vs.
AN ARMY OF THUGS!

"Gotcha, freak!" shouted one of the hoodlums.

Then he and his fellow goons went flying as if a land mine had exploded beneath them. Spider-Man was back on his feet, ready to meet the next rush through the door.

A bloodthirsty crowd jammed the doorway. Then Borloff heard more screeching and shouting from outside, and Daredevil rocketed in—right over the heads of the mass of thugs blocking the entrance.

"Thought I'd find you here," Daredevil said, hurling some of the flattened hoods into the mass of attackers.

"Yeah, that crowd in the street was a dead giveaway," Spider-Man said. As he spoke, his left fist connected with three jaws in quick succession. His right wrist threw webbing over another half-dozen of Hell's Kitchen's fiercest street thugs.

DEADLY CURE

Bill McCay
Illustrations by John Nyberg

BYRON PREISS MULTIMEDIA COMPANY, INC.
NEW YORK

POCKET BOOKS
NEW YORK   LONDON   TORONTO   SYDNEY   TOKYO   SINGAPORE

This book is a work of fiction. Names, characters, places and incidents are products of the author's imagination or are used fictitiously. Any resemblance to actual events or locales or persons, living or dead, is entirely coincidental.

An *Original* Publication of POCKET BOOKS

POCKET BOOKS, a division of Simon & Schuster Inc.
1230 Avenue of the Americas, New York, NY 10020

Copyright © 1996 Marvel Characters, Inc.
A Byron Preiss Multimedia Company, Inc. Book

Byron Preiss Multimedia Company, Inc.
24 West 25th Street
New York, New York 10010

The Byron Preiss Multimedia Worldwide Wed Site Address is:
http://www.byronpreiss.com

ISBN 0-671-00320-8

First Pocket Books paperback printing August 1996

10 9 8 7 6 5 4 3 2 1

POCKET and colophon are registered trademarks of Simon & Schuster Inc.

Edited by Howard Zimmerman
Cover art by Mike Zeck and Phil Zimelman
Cover design by Claude Goodwin
Interior design by MM Design 2000, Inc.

Printed in the U.S.A.

To Mom—without her, this book would have
been short an author.
&
To Stan Lee—without him, this book would
have been short a lot of characters.

B.McC

ACKNOWLEDGMENTS

Special thanks for grace under fire during the production of this book goes to: Dave Stern at Pocket Books; Stacy Gittelman, Steve Behling, John Conroy and Mike Thomas at Marvel Creative Services; Keith R. A. DeCandido and Steve Roman at BPMC; designer Claude Goodwin; Dan Faust at Jackson Typesetting; and artists John Nyberg, Mike Zeck and Phil Zimelman.

SPIDER-MAN
SUPER THRILLER
— DEADLY CURE —

CHAPTER

—1—

W hat was *that?*" The mugger's vicious smile quickly faded as he looked up. His eyes widened and he almost dropped the three-foot length of pipe in his hand.

Spider-Man had seen it all before. Thugs all looked alike when they spotted a red-and-blue figure sweeping down a wall at them.

The punk turned from the elderly woman he had cornered. With a wild yell, he swung the pipe awkwardly over his head at Spidey. Metal clanged against the brick of the alley wall as he missed the masked super hero.

Spider-Man braked with one hand on the wall, lashing out with the other. He was used to fighting at this angle. *Crack!* Even as his fist connected with the thief's jaw, his spider-sense warned him of another threat.

Spider-Man turned to face a second mugger, who had been hiding in the shadows of the alley.

"Hey," the first thug whined as he tried unsuccessfully to get up. "You can't do that. We got rights—"

"How about your victim—that helpless woman you shoved in here?" Spider-Man asked. "Didn't she have rights?"

The woman had shown the spunk and grit of a true New Yorker. As soon as the muggers had been distracted, she'd gotten out of there.

Waving his knife with false courage, the second punk came at Spidey. "I'm gonna cut—"

Thwip! Spider-Man triggered one of his web-shooters. A stream of silken goo jetted out, gluing the young man's left hand to the wall behind him. With a squawk, the thug bounced back to the wall. He slashed at the webbing with his knife, trying to free his other hand.

"That won't work," Spidey warned. "Unless you're willing to cut off your hand . . ."

The guy whipped round to face the hero, waving his blade wildly.

Spider-Man shot webbing at the mugger's knife-hand and glued that to the wall, too.

Straining and kicking, the young thug tried

to break free. Spidey waited until the guy had a foot up at an uncomfortable angle and webbed that into place, too.

"You won't get away with this," the thug snarled. "We ain't alone—"

"Oh? You and your pal on the ground are members of the New York Low-Lifes Union?" Spider-Man drawled. "What are you gonna do? Picket me?"

"We're connected," the punk told him. "Hooked up with the big guy. *You* know who I mean."

"You two? Working for the Kingpin?" Spider-Man laughed. "Give me a break."

"Broken leg—or a broken neck!" The thug's threats would have been scarier if he hadn't been webbed up and hanging half off the side of the building. "We're gonna—glomph!"

Tired of the ranting, Spider-Man fired a stream of webbing across the guy's mouth.

"You just hang there quietly, while I web up your friend and leave you for the cops," the super hero said. Finishing with the other mugger, he fired a web-line to the cornice of one of the buildings that closed in the alley. Hauling himself up, he shot another web-strand to a tenement across the street.

He paused for a second to reload his web-shooters. *Which way?* Spider-Man asked himself, scanning the nearly empty sidewalks. He had no target, no place he had to be. This was the boring part of the super hero business, going on patrol.

With a shrug, Spider-Man turned west. Soon he'd left behind the mean streets of lower Manhattan for the quiet lanes of Greenwich Village.

There was some bustle in the complex of buildings known as Empire State University. Spider-Man swung to the top of a dorm that overlooked the block-square park in the center of ESU.

Not so long ago, he'd been a student there, as slightly nerdy Peter Parker. He could have been one of the kids leaving the Science Center after a late class . . .

Spider-Man stiffened as he glanced over to the towering, white-brick building that housed the university's science department. His nerves seemed to jangle, as if an invisible hand were plucking at them. The sensation intensified into a dentist-drill buzzing in his brain. His spider-sense was screaming a warning of *danger! danger!* connected with the science building.

Tensed for action, Spider-Man looked hard at the building entrance. A big, thick-bodied man was making his way in. The students seemed to part around him like a stream of water flowing around a rock. A new jangle of warning buzzed in the hero's head.

Spidey leapt from rooftop to rooftop, making his way around the square of buildings fronting the park. Even as he moved, he could feel the sensation of danger coming closer.

Spider-Man reached the science building and scampered down the wall. Urged on by the danger warning pounded through his head, he didn't care if anyone spotted him against the white bricks. He halted by a window mid-way down and stared inside. He saw a large room and three men.

Spidey knew this place. It was the big, untidy laboratory where Professor Aron Esterhazy conducted his experiments. He remembered thinking that the professor looked like a stork in his white lab coat—beaky nose, thick glasses with heavy black frames, his white hair rising in untidy tufts like feathers. Esterhazy was a true head-in-the-clouds type. The students jokingly called him "Professor Hazy." But even though he was world-famous in biogenetics, the professor still taught beginning courses. Peter Parker had studied with him, had learned much from him and liked the man.

There was nothing at all to like about the squat, hard-faced man who faced Esterhazy. He barely glanced at the lab animals the professor was trying to show him. "My files show how the formula has improved each of these subjects," Esterhazy said.

The troll-like man cut him off. "Wait—get rid of your pal here."

"Certainly, Mister, ah, Smith." Esterhazy's voice was nervous as he turned to the other scientist in the room. Spider-Man recognized him immediately. The short beard edging the man's round face was grayer, but Esterhazy's lab wouldn't be the same without Dr. David Borloff. He had studied with the famous professor, then gone to work for him many years ago.

Some people in the science department said Borloff was more like Dr. Hazy's son than his assistant. Certainly, the veteran researcher always followed Esterhazy's orders. He left immediately.

"Does he know about your research?" Mr. Smith demanded.

"Only certain of the early stages," Esterhazy answered. "He helped me review the available information on the military's attempts to create a *super soldier*. Of course, my goal is different. My formula will bring subjects to their full genetic potential—a step beyond the military's goals."

"Speaking of the next step," the hard-faced

stranger said, "we lined up some guys to try your formula out—"

Esterhazy looked shocked. "It's far too soon for human testing. It's not safe yet. I couldn't—"

"You'll have to, Doc. We can make you." Smith reached into his coat. At the window, Spider-Man tensed. He'd noticed the bulge inside the man's jacket before. But there was no new tingle from his spider-sense, so he stayed where he was.

The thuggish man's hand only brought out a piece of paper from his inner pocket. "Here's a copy of your funding agreement. It says that *we* own the research."

Esterhazy grabbed for the paper. "I never agreed—"

"You sure did, Doc. Maybe you missed seeing it in your hurry to sign after your government grant ended. But it's right here, in black and white."

"The foundation would never—"

"Hey—it may say 'foundation' in these papers, but the money comes from one guy. And he's got leg-breakers—er, *volunteers*—who need your formula to reach their full genetic whatchamacallit."

"You can't seriously expect me to follow your orders."

"Not *my* orders." Smith's face formed the

barest of smiles. "They come from my boss—the guy who owns your formula."

"No!" Esterhazy snatched up a test tube from a rack on the lab table. To Spidey, he looked like a man trying to rescue a favorite child from danger.

"Jerk!" A backhand blow from the heavy-set Smith knocked Esterhazy to the floor.

Now Spider-Man made his move, smashing through the window to save the professor. Glass flew everywhere, covering the still figure on the floor. Spidey saw blood.

Great, he thought, *I've sliced up poor Dr. Hazy.* Then he saw that the blood came from the professor's hand, which still clutched the now-broken test tube.

"Yo, Spider-freak!" The harsh lines of Smith's face grew even harder as he backed up. "You got no call to come busting in like that. I'm just doing some business with the professor, here. He owes my boss—"

The man's hand darted under his coat. This time Spider-Man didn't wait for a warning from his spider-sense. He knew the man was reaching for a gun. Spidey charged forward to nail Smith, just as the buzz of his spider-sense shrilled a warning—from *behind* him.

Spidey whirled. Esterhazy lay twitching on the tiles, seemingly in agony.

He looks awful! But that smack he took

wasn't enough to do this, Spider-Man thought. *So why—?*

At that moment, an unearthly scream came from the professor, freezing Smith and Spider-Man for the moment.

Spidey glanced back to the broken vial in the professor's cut hand. *The formula must be getting into Esterhazy's bloodstream,* he realized. Like it or not, the professor's invention was receiving a human test.

"Aaargh! Nnnngh!" Esterhazy cried through clenched teeth. He huddled on his hands and knees. And all of a sudden, the baggy lab coat that had swum around the professor began bursting at the seams.

The tall, weedy man abruptly grew a muscular pair of shoulders. They strained the white cloth, tearing it apart.

Esterhazy rose to his feet, lurching forward. The sleeves of his coat ripped, revealing arms like a sumo wrestler's. The new Esterhazy wasn't quite in the same league as the incredible Hulk, but his muscular explosion was most impressive.

Smith was still frozen with one hand inside his coat. "Whoa," he said in a soft voice.

Esterhazy lunged for the thug. He grabbed the guy, picking him right off the floor. Rather than stopping him, Spider-Man decided to see what the transformed professor had in mind.

The hood's eyes glittered with panic as he battered at the monstrously muscled professor. Esterhazy's glasses flew off, but otherwise the guy might as well have been punching a statue.

Esterhazy tossed the man aside like a piece of paper. He turned to the lab table and began smashing everything on it.

"Wha—what are you doing?" Spider-Man demanded.

"Depriving this dog's master of my work," the raging Esterhazy coldly replied. "He may have the law on his side—but he will *not* have my formula."

The professor turned from the table to a computer on a desk. "I kept no records of my research—except in here." He pressed buttons on the keyboard. "Now it's erased—blanked without hope of recovery. And these are the backups."

Esterhazy scooped up a couple of computer disks, and Spider-Man's warning sense began tingling like mad.

"Stop it—you're crazy!" Smith leapt to his feet, his hand again going for his gun.

The professor crushed the disks in one hand, just as—

Thwip! Spider-Man fired off his web-shooters

All of a sudden, the baggy lab coat that had swum around the professor began bursting at the seams.

at the thug's hand, which now held a revolver. The heavy pistol was instantly enveloped in a globe of webbing. Furious, Smith tried to fire—although he looked like he was aiming a pillow at the professor.

When the gun didn't go off, Smith went wild and charged Spider-Man. The ball of webbing that encased Smith's hand caught the hero in the face, knocking him back.

Spidey braced himself, shoving Smith away and clipping him hard with a left-right combination. A buzz of warning from his spidersense held him back from finishing the thug. Spider-Man turned in time to see Dr. Esterhazy running from the lab.

"Do you think he needs to feed the parking meter on his car?" Spidey asked the thug who was struggling to free himself from the super hero's grip.

Without waiting for an answer, Spider-Man dug out a spider-tracer and tossed it like a frisbee. His aim was true. The homing device stuck to the back of Esterhazy's tattered lab coat. Spidey then turned his attention back to the thuggish Mr. Smith. It took only another minute to finish off the hoodlum and leave him securely webbed to the laboratory floor.

Spider-Man had taken only three steps down the hallway where Esterhazy had fled when he came face-to-face with Dr. Borloff.

The professor's round face went pale with fear. "Leave me alone!" he screamed. "What did you do to Aron! Aron? What's going on?" Before Spider-Man could reply, Borloff's fist smacked a fire alarm box on the wall, and all hell broke loose.

"Oops," Spidey said, "wrong door. I was looking for the *lavatory*, not the laboratory."

He spun, exiting the lab the same way he'd entered—through the broken window. It was better than trying to get down the stairs before university security arrived.

Spider-Man clung to the wall of the science building, trying to track the signal from the vanished professor.

There it was—in the park below. *Old Dr. Hazy must be moving pretty quickly to get that far this fast*, Spidey thought.

Spider-Man flicked a line of webbing and swung down to treetop level. Dr. Esterhazy seemed to be headed toward Sixth Avenue. As Spidey went hurtling in that direction, though, the tracer's signal suddenly shifted to the south.

Thwip! Another line of webbing was fired—a veering course change. But as Spidey moved, the tracer was suddenly heading north.

What's up, Doc? Spidey wondered. *Why are you doubling back?* He landed in the upper branches of a tree, straining his senses to get a closer fix on the spider-tracer. Doc Hazy was up in the trees now. "What's the old guy doing—his Tarzan impression?" Spider-Man muttered to himself.

The fix swerved again, then yet again. With mounting frustration, Spidey set off on a zig-zag chase around the park. Students stopped, pointing, yelling as they detected Spider-Man among the tree branches.

Spidey thought they'd have an easier time spotting a flying professor in a tattered white lab coat.

According to his spider-sense, the tracer was now climbing the side of the stone archway at the entrance to the park. But Spider-Man couldn't spot the scrambling professor.

Is this the next step in genetics? the puzzled hero wondered. *Invisibility?*

Firing off another web-line, he swung to the top of the arch, intercepting the tracer—and its wearer.

Behind the lenses of his mask, Spider-Man's eyes widened. There wasn't any professor to be found. He'd been tracking . . . a squirrel. The tracer had been stuck into the thick fur on its back.

"I guess the professor *is* getting improved," he muttered. "The old Doc Hazy would never have thought of *this* trick!"

CHAPTER

—2—

The office tower rose high into the sky, dwarfing the other midtown Manhattan buildings around it. As far as the public knew, it was the headquarters of a man who imported spices for a living.

In truth, it was the nerve center of an empire, a network of legal and illegal activities that criss-crossed the city, bringing the metropolis under the control of one man ... a man known as the Kingpin of crime.

Floor-to-ceiling glass panels offered the cityscape as a panoramic view—a glimpse of his domain. His office was large, his desk big enough to park a car on. Yet, just as his tower dwarfed the nearby office buildings, the Kingpin himself made the office furniture look small. His bald head was egg-shaped, spreading out at its base onto a short, thick neck, so that his face seemed thrust forward at the world, like a bull's. The Kingpin's body seemed to swell out into huge shoulders, arms like tree-trunks, a big belly that was mostly muscle, and massive legs.

Although he was clad in a perfectly tailored white suit, there was an air of grossness to the Kingpin—a feeling of "too much." The amount of material that went into making his fancy embroidered vest would have been enough to make a whole suit for a normal man.

But the Kingpin was not a normal man. Despite his overweight look, there was always a hunger in his eyes, a desire that could be summed up in one word: *more*.

The windows showed the distant city lights in the darkness. Their glow added to the illumination in the office as the Kingpin watched the sorry-looking figure before him. A platoon of lawyers had quickly gotten his lieutenant, Mr. Smith, out of police custody. The lump of webbing had just dissolved, and the bruises on the man's face were still fresh as he gave his report.

". . . so, I finally had to get physical with Esterhazy. But when I did, Spider-Man came busting through the window."

The Kingpin nodded. "That wall-crawling

annoyance has already disrupted this project once before. To improve our—negotiating stance—with Dr. Esterhazy, I had ordered that the professor's wife be *secured* as my guest. Spider-Man interrupted that operation. I've had to dispatch a new team to *invite* Mrs. Esterhazy."

"Is that how Spider-Man found out about the professor?" A look of concern filled the thug's battered features.

"Unlikely," Kingpin responded dryly. "The operatives had no knowledge as to who Mrs. Esterhazy was."

"Then how—?"

Kingpin made a dismissing gesture. "It sometimes seems that coincidence is the stock in trade of the so-called super heroes. I'm more interested in the effects of the formula on the professor."

His lieutenant shrugged, then winced. "You can see 'em on my face, sir. That old guy bounced me around like a basketball."

The Kingpin's eyebrows rose. "I thought your bruises came from Spider-Man. If the feeble Dr. Esterhazy did that, his formula could indeed help create a superior—how did you put it?—leg-breaker."

He tapped the intercom on his desk. "Bring in the Esterhazy file."

An executive assistant immediately appeared with a file folder. The Kingpin sifted through the papers inside. Here was the funding agreement between Aron Esterhazy and the foundation the Kingpin had set up through dummy corporations. Ah—and the report on possible pressure points to be used against the professor. The man was dedicated to his work—he almost didn't have an outside life.

But there was a wife, even if she had recently divorced him. The Kingpin picked up a photograph from the file—a round-faced, bearded man. "David Borloff," he read, "a former student of the professor's, now a fellow worker. I think it would be worthwhile to put a watch on him. Dr. Esterhazy is on the run—he may turn to his friend for help."

The Kingpin leaned back in his seat, steepling his fingers. "Which brings us to the problem of the wandering Esterhazy. I want all of our street-level operatives—even those incompetents who tried to snatch *Mrs.* Esterhazy—on alert."

He removed another photo from the file— a surveillance shot of Esterhazy. "Have this copied and distributed. If anyone sees Esterhazy, they are to bring him in."

The somewhat battered lieutenant took the picture from his boss. "He's not gonna come easily, sir. How far can the boys go to bring him down?"

"I want Esterhazy *alive*." The Kingpin's voice was firm. "But that doesn't mean he has to come in—unhurt."

With a nod, the thug took the second photo. "I'll see to it right away, sir."

He turned to the office door, but before he reached it, the heavy wooden panel swung inward. A woman stood in the doorway, her dark hair a tousled cloud around her delicate face. There were traces of gray around her temples, but she was still breathtakingly beautiful. Her eyes were dark—and strangely empty. The intruder stood barefoot on the thick carpet, a bathrobe wrapped around an expensive, long silk nightgown.

"Um, uh, good evening Mrs.—uh—"

The tough guy's voice died as the woman's blank gaze focused on him. Her face turned into a mask of fright.

The face the thug turned to his boss was almost as fear-filled. The Kingpin had a short way with people who got on his bad side. And the easiest way to the big man's bad side was by upsetting his wife.

With a silent flick of his eyes, the Kingpin dismissed his lieutenant. The man hastily got out as his boss rose behind the masssive desk.

"Vanessa, dear, what a pleasant surprise."

The gentleness in the Kingpin's voice couldn't have been more different from the cold tones he'd used a moment ago.

His wife didn't say a word, but he could read her face. She turned from the scary man by the door to give her husband a shy smile. For the Kingpin, that smile was like a knife in the heart. There was no recognition in Vanessa's eyes. She didn't see him as her husband. She was only smiling at the nice man with the kind voice.

The Kingpin held out his hand, struggling to keep it and his voice level. "Come here, Vanessa."

She came to him immediately, childlike trust on her face.

Over the years, the Kingpin had seen many expressions on Vanessa's face. There was the terror and confusion when she'd first been brought to him, a beautiful young woman with amnesia. He'd been plain Willie Fisk then, leader of a street gang. But even then, he'd been struck by her beauty—her innocence.

He'd wanted her by his side . . . and gotten her. But as he moved from success to success in the world of crime, Wilson Fisk had seen other emotions on Vanessa's face. Disappointment. Doubt. Fear.

Then her mind had fled into this unknown

illness, leaving a wan, silent innocent behind—a child who stared at him with
stranger's eyes.

How fitting that she should appear as he
was discussing what to do with Dr. Esterhazy.
Vanessa was the real reason that the Kingpin
had financed the professor's research. The
dummy foundation had bankrolled several
medical and biogenetic projects. Esterhazy's
formula was the first of all these efforts to
bear fruit.

*Certainly, the formula helped the doctor
when he was threatened,* the Kingpin thought.
Could it heal the scars in Vanessa's mind?

She stood beside him now, slipping her
hand into his. Her delicate fingers seemed lost
in his massive palm, engulfed to the wrist in
the clasp of his bearlike paw.

"We'll go for a walk," he said in a kind,
low voice.

Slowly, moving as though he carried something incredibly fragile, the Kingpin brought
Vanessa to an elevator. He talked as they
journeyed, filling the silence.

They rode upward as the Kingpin gently
reprimanded her for going off alone. The elevator doors opened on a scene of confusion
when the reached the floor that held Vanessa's suite of rooms.

A doctor, several nurses and a pair of bodyguards were rushing around like chickens with their heads cut off. When the doctor saw who accompanied the Kingpin, his face went as white as the coat he wore.

"M-Mister Fisk," he nearly gobbled in fear. "I was just about to call you—"

"No, you weren't. You were hoping your people would find my wife before it became necessary to inform me that you'd *lost* her." The Kingpin loomed over the doctor—a new specialist he'd brought in—ready to express his displeasure.

Beside him, Vanessa flinched at his tone of voice. The nice man was becoming not-nice now.

The Kingpin turned to his wife, his voice a little hoarse as he tried to throttle his rage. "Why don't you go with the nice nurse, my dear? She'll make you—comfortable."

One of the nurses came forward while the other began preparing a hypodermic needle. Both of them and the guards had large, phony smiles plastered on their faces—and sweat on their brows.

With a little sigh, Vanessa let herself be coaxed away.

The Kingpin turned to the doctor. There was no need to mince words. "You allowed my wife to wander about unattended. She could have been hurt."

The Kingpin loomed over the doctor—a new specialist he'd brought in—ready to express his displeasure.

"A shocking oversight," the ashen-faced doctor babbled. "Believe me, I'll shake up the staff—"

"Do that," the Kingpin cut him off. "And remember, I hold *you* personally responsible. Your predecessor grew careless . . . so careless, he finally had an accident."

"A-accident?" the doctor faltered.

"He fell out of one of the top-story windows."

The doctor looked confused. "B-but those windows don't open."

"Yes," the Kingpin said as he turned away. "A shocking oversight."

People in Hell's Kitchen didn't tend to look toward the sky. There were too many unpleasant things on the street that might be stepped on. And there were too many unpleasant people ready to step on anyone who didn't pay attention.

So no one noticed that one of the old brick tenements seemed to have suddenly grown a blood-red gargoyle. It was a horned human figure who knelt unnaturally still on the roof line. Daredevil would have known if anyone had commented on his appearance. He was straining his enhanced hearing, sorting through the sounds of the street below.

Sometimes, hearing the street buzz was like

listening to music—the jazz beat of a big city. Tonight, though, there was too much ugly noise. Heckling, threats—the sounds of pained elderly voices.

The rows of old buildings were home to a surprising number of older people. Many had grown up in Hell's Kitchen when it had been a working-man's district, lawless but vibrant. The factories had gone, the neighborhood faded—but retirees clung to small apartments with cheap rents. And there were many who saw the elderly as easy targets.

"Shut up, Grandpa!" a nasty voice sneered in the near distance.

"If I were ten years younger—" a hoarse, old man's voice quavered.

"Maybe I should just finish you off!"

Daredevil was already moving toward the altercation when he heard a new voice cut in. "C'mon, Johnny, that's not the old guy we want."

"Lucky for him," Johnny muttered.

Daredevil detected the sound of feet moving away. He stopped to monitor the victim's condition. His radar sense showed the old man leaning against the boarded-up windows of an abandoned store. He could hear the man breathing heavily, his weak heart thumping in his chest. But he seemed all right.

Frowning, Daredevil set off after the street gang that had cornered the old man. Something was up. The street gangs seemed especially interested in going after elderly men tonight. Half a dozen times, he'd either heard or interrupted—what? They weren't exactly attacks. The gangs seemed to be conducting identity checks.

"Whoa, what happened here?"

Daredevil heard the sneering voice of the gang member named Johnny. He listened more carefully, catching the sounds of groans. Scanning the street ahead, he "saw" that two groups of thugs had met. From the way they moved and the sounds they made, one crew had taken a pretty bad pounding.

"You guys see a big old coot in a torn-up white coat?" one of the newcomers asked. He sounded as if he were talking with a split lip. "Watch out for him. He's a strong mother."

Daredevil set off across the rooftops, leaving the young thugs behind. This wasn't the first gang who'd tangled with an oldster who'd messed them up. Daredevil had come across several groups like that tonight.

There was more to be found out. And Daredevil knew exactly where . . .

Josie's place was a cheap bar down by the old seaport, the part that tourists don't visit. Daredevil knew he was coming close because the stink of stale beer drowned out the brackish smell of the harbor water. From time to time, he'd had to bust into Josie's and thump a few heads to get some information.

He didn't have to do it this time, though. Through the plate-glass window, a voice came to his super-sensitive ears.

"Awright, getcha brains off them seats and into the streets. This ain't me talkin', the word's come down from the big man."

There was only one "big man" in local crime circles: the Kingpin.

Daredevil listened to the rustle of papers. "This is a picture of a guy the boss wants. If ya see him . . . get him. So long as he's breathing when you bring him in."

"This is the picture of an old guy!" another voice burst out. "What's the big cheese want with him?"

"Maybe he owes money for his dentures—I dunno," the messenger replied. "Maybe you'll find out if you deliver him."

Daredevil heard the rattle of glasses, the creaks and clatter of chairs being shoved back.

"You're emptying my place!" A woman's voice, shrill and hoarse from too many cigarettes rose in complaint. "You're worse than that guy in the red suit."

"Yeah," came the answer. "Daredevil never

burned your place down. That might happen if you don't shut your yap."

Daredevil disappeared into the night. He had a lot to think about. Why were so many street toughs being used to find a single old man, and bring him to Daredevil's old enemy, the Kingpin?

CHAPTER

—3—

The warm, stale air of Grand Central Station felt as if it had been breathed and re-breathed about a thousand times. Down the hallways deep below the ground, there was no way to telling day from night.

But it was definitely morning. Thousands of commuters were marching through on the way to their jobs above.

An old-fashioned telephone booth, one that still had a door, stood at the foot of a rampway. The door rattled open and a white-haired man rambled out. He wore a dark wool overcoat that was too small for him. The hem barely reached his knees, and four inches of wrist stuck out of the sleeves. One lapel seemed to have been torn off, and the man's left knee could be seen through a tear in his pants.

The passing stream of travelers split around him as though he had the plague. The people on the way to work didn't want to hassle with a homeless person. Sometimes they go violent . . .

The passengers also detoured around a group of hard-eyed young men in leather jackets at the top of the ramp. "Hey Knucks," one of the thugs suddenly said "That old geezer down there. Doesn't he look like the guy in the picture?"

Digging out a crumpled piece of paper, the leader of the group held it out in a big, hairy paw. "Maybe," Knucks said. "If the dude had put on about thirty pounds and hadn't shaved for a couple of days."

He shrugged. "Let's get down with the guy."

The white-haired man saw the five punks coming down the ramp toward him. He glanced right and left, as the travelers carefully avoiding his eyes. Then he put down his head and charged.

The first two thugs were caught flat-footed. The old guy grabbed them by their leather jackets and flung them into the walls. Commuters broke into a mad scramble as flying bodies landed among them like bombs.

Knucks slipped his trademark brass knuckles out of his pocket and took a swing. His

yes went big as the white-haired dude
ucked with the agility of a much younger
man and counter-punched. Knucks hit the
oor and shook his head.

"I'd say this is *definitely* the guy," he
croaked as he spat out a bloody, broken
ooth.

The two remaining members of the crew
:apt to grab the old man's arms. He shook
imself free of one gang member, but then
he two guys he'd decked waded back into
he fight. One twined his hands together and
lubbed down on the old man's shoulder. The
low staggered the old coot just as Knucks
icked the back of the man's knee. Down
vent the old guy, with one of the crew leap-
ng on his back.

"Keep him down!" Knucks yelled, rising up
n his knees and drawing back his weighted
st. He brought it down hard, hoping to rack
p the guy's head, but good.

The old dude heaved up, swinging the guy
n his back right into the punch Knucks
vas throwing.

Without a sound, the punk landed bone-
essly on the floor. His eyes had rolled up in
is head.

"Oh, *man!*" Knucks burst out. "Hold him,
uys! Keep him down!"

But their intended victim would not be

held. With a deep, wordless roar, he came up off the floor, shedding the three guys trying to bulldog him as if they were dandruff. Two were still holding onto one arm. The third member of the crew had wrapped himself around the guy's legs, trying to tackle him.

"This is it, Gramps!" an infuriated Knuck yelled. "I'm taking you down!"

The white-haired man looked hardly grandfatherly as he kicked away the punk clinging to his legs. Half his ragged overcoat tore away as he escaped the tormentors trying to hold him.

Knucks swung, only to have his blow knocked aside by an arm like a tree limb. He saw a bony fist come zooming toward his face. Then, everything went dark.

Spider-Man opened the pouch of webbing where he'd left his street clothes and quickly assumed the identity of Peter Parker. The sun was up, and the streets were beginning to fill with people on their way to work. He joined the passing parade till he found a working pay phone.

It was time to call his wife.

Mary Jane should be up by now, and she'd be concerned that he hadn't come home. She was pretty good about the strange schedule a super hero sometimes had to follow. But

He came up off the floor, shedding the three guys trying to bulldog him as if they were dandruff.

Peter knew that the dangers he faced worried his wife. She'd want to know he hadn't been beaten to a pulp and left in an alley somewhere.

He phoned home, holding on the line for four rings. Could MJ be in the shower or something?

Then their answering machine picked up. The tape wasn't their usual message. Mary Jane's voice sounded tight and a little flustered as she asked callers to leave their number and a message. "And if this is Peter, you know what to dial for a special message."

Feeling a little numb, Peter punched the special code on the pay-phone buttons. A new tape came on. "Hey, hon, I hate to tell you like this, but you're out, and the phone rang—your aunt isn't feeling well. I'll be with her out in Forest Hills. Call me there. Bye!"

Peter Parker had a familiar empty feeling in the pit of his stomach. His aunt was all the family he had, anymore. She and his Uncle Ben had taken care of him when his parents had died. Then Uncle Ben had been killed . . . and Peter had become Spider-Man. Aunt May had grown older and more frail. Even something mild like a cold or the flu could do a number on her.

More change came out of Peter's pocket as he dialed a phone number in Queens.

"Hello," a familiar voice answered.

Peter smiled. Even over the phone, he could feel the personality of his lovely red-haired wife.

"MJ, it's Peter. Everything okay?"

"Petey—" A sigh of relief came over the phone. "Aunt May has come down with some sort of bug. The doctor was a little worried, so I decided to stay over. She doesn't want me to 'fuss over her' as she put it." Mary Jane hesitated for a moment. "But she's awfully weak. I think she'd be glad to see you. I know I would."

It was Peter's turn to sigh. "Right now, I can't," he said. "I'm trying to find someone— to help them. But I'll be there as soon as I can. That's a promise."

"Okay," Mary Jane said, but she didn't sound happy. "I've managed to switch around my schedule, so I'll be out here if you need me."

"Hey, I always need you. See you soon."

"I hope so," Mary Jane said.

Peter hung up the phone, feeling the time seem to rush around him. He'd wasted a night trying to find Dr. Esterhazy. All he'd found was a lot of low-lifes hassling older people. And there was still the problem of how to help the professor once he found him.

Maybe Spidey or Peter Parker can't help,

but I know someone who could. He stepped away from the pay phone and headed for the nearest alley. *Better to make this visit in costume,* he thought. *Besides, swinging my way there will save the carfare.*

Matt Murdock's law office wasn't the fancy type that people saw on TV. Some of his clients would tell him that, then stop in embarrassment. Matt Murdock had never seen a television lawyer's office. Matt Murdock was blind.

He'd smile and say they should be glad— they'd know he'd be working on their cases and not goofing off in front of the tube.

Most clients figured that blindness was the reason for the Spartan simplicity of the office—two chairs facing a desk with a third chair. A blind man wouldn't want to have a lot of things that got in his way. That was true, though not of Murdock. Matt could "see" everything in the room with an uncanny radar sense. His hearing was so super-sharp, he could tune in on people's heartbeats. His touch was so sensitive, his fingers could read" the inked letters printed on a newspaper.

Matt Murdock had been blinded by a radioactive isotope spilling from a truck. But that glowing sludge had given him these other, strange senses for the one it had stolen. Matt Murdock was not a person to be pitied.

He was the superpowered avenger known as Daredevil.

As he opened his empty office, Murdock frowned in thought, still trying to piece together the odd bits of information he'd picked up the night before. He headed to the window and halted. The faintest *swish* in the air currents outside told of a body swinging down from the roof. The powerful pumping of the heart revealed the swinger's identity—Spider-Man.

Murdock threw the window open. "Get in here quickly before someone sees you."

"And the happiest of howdies to *you*, DD," Spider-Man sourly replied. The two heroes had known each others' secret identities for years, but that didn't mean they were friends. As far as Daredevil was concerned, Spider-Man was an exuberant kid. He had no idea of planning, of picking his fights. He just wanted to go in swinging.

Spider-Man considered the older hero a bit of a stick-in-the-mud . . . and not always a person to be completely trusted.

"What do you want?" Murdock asked abruptly.

"I have a friend who needs legal advice," Spider-Man said. "He's a scientist at ESU. But he got tied up with some nasty types who put up money for his research—"

At first, Murdock listened to the story with impatience. But when he heard of Esterhazy's transformation, he began to get interested.

"It was more than just muscles," Spider-Man went on. "Dr. Hazy was blind as a bat without his glasses. But when this creep knocked them off, the professor could see just fine."

Murdock felt a jump in his own heartbeat. *A genetic formula that restores perfect vision* . . .

The thought was pushed away as pieces fit together in Murdock's head. An old man with something the Kingpin wanted. Thugs out combing the streets for an elderly type. Dr. Esterhazy beating up on the man who'd come to threaten him. Search parties being thrashed . . .

"This professor is in deeper than you know," Murdock spoke up. "The money for that research came from the Kingpin."

"You're kidding!" Spider-Man burst out.

"I've heard the street punks putting out the word," Murdock said. "It came directly from the top. With the Kingpin after him, Esterhazy needs more than legal advice. He'll need to be found—and protected."

"Sure," Spider-Man said bitterly. "Let's find and *hide* Esterhazy. We certainly can't go and rattle the Kingpin's cage."

Murdock sighed. He'd had this argument often enough with the younger hero. "As far as the law is concerned, Wilson Fisk is a respectable businessman."

"Yeah—so what if we know that Fatboy Fisk is also the Kingpin of Crime?" Spider-Man almost slammed a fist down on Murdock's desk, then stopped.

Just as well, Daredevil thought. *Given the mood he's in, he'd have broken it.*

"What about that gun-toting thug he sent to steal the professor's work?" Spidey snarled.

Daredevil shrugged. "First, we can't prove the Kingpin sent him. Second, if Esterhazy's funding came from the Kingpin, Fisk could hardly be accused of *stealing* the work—could he?

"I don't have to like it," Daredevil continued. "But the Kingpin has never been tied into anything illegal. Until we can get the proof to put him away—"

"By that time that happens—if ever—I'll be an old man," Spider-Man complained. "And Dr. Esterhazy will probably end up feeding the fishes. The prof needs help *now.*"

The impatience of youth, Daredevil thought.

"I know, but the Kingpin does seem to have the law on his side," Murdock said. "He's got a contract with Esterhazy. Maybe the research itself is illegal—or the substances the professor was working with. If we could prove that, we might be able to pressure the Kingpin into letting Esterhazy off the hook."

"But that'll take time, DD. I'd prefer applying pressure directly to fatso's throat! Maybe if we put a hurt on him—"

"We'd be just like he is!" Daredevil said. "Besides, that kind of pressure will only make him send out twice as many goons to collect Esterhazy."

Spider-Man sighed. "I don't know ... maybe you're right. But—look, Doc Hazy is a friend. He's a brilliant man who taught me a lot," Spidey said. "I came here hoping you could *help* me—"

The blind lawyer shrugged again. "There may be some legal avenues to explore, as I said. But first I have to have a client."

He began slipping off his street clothes, revealing the red suit of the Daredevil. "If we can find Esterhazy first, we may have a chance."

CHAPTER

—4—

Sunlight poured through the curving glass walls of the Kingpin's private solarium. It was high enough that no other buildings could cast a shadow on it. The warmth and soft glow of the sun made the enclosed balcony feel like a bubble of spring in the midst of winter.

But the sunshine could not melt the ball of ice encasing the Kingpin's heart as he sat with his wife.

He took his usual care to move slowly, to speak pleasantly, even tenderly. Vanessa gave her usual empty smile to the nice man.

The Kingpin took out something from the pocket of his white jacket. It was a little image made of crystal—a portrait of Vanessa. Once it had been a sign of their love. Several times, the crystal had been battered in battles with self-righteous costumed heroes. The Kingpin had been forced to send to Europe to find a craftsman who could make repairs.

Vanessa gave a cry of wordless delight when she saw the pretty thing. She held it up so the crystal could catch the light, smiling and cooing.

She didn't recognize that the image was her own face. Vanessa didn't recognize anyone in her life.

The Kingpin wasn't sure whether he wanted to smash the crystal portrait or laugh out loud. Surely the fates must be chuckling if they looked down on this scene. He sat on a balcony, the king of all he surveyed. Nothing in this city—in the world—could stop him from taking a single thing he wanted.

But the thing he wanted most—the soul of the woman he loved—eluded all of his power and ingenuity.

With firm but gentle fingers, he took back the crystal carving. Vanessa tried to resist, reaching out to the crystal, pouting.

"Vanessa—no!" the Kingpin burst out in annoyance.

Vanessa's face clouded with fear, and she huddled in upon herself.

Wilson Fisk gritted his teeth. With two

words, he had managed to wreck the afternoon.

"No, dear," he said soothingly. "Let me keep this. I'll bring it to you tomorrow."

The look she gave him was the nervous glance of a wild animal, not sure if the stranger will be kind—or attack. Trying to give Vanessa a reassuring smile, the Kingpin rose to his feet. "Nurse," he called.

A nurse immediately appeared at the balcony entrance.

"I'll see you again—very soon," the Kingpin promised.

As usual, there was no response—no goodbye.

He stepped into the luxurious apartment that made up Vanessa's quarters, still looking at the crystal image, at a Vanessa who was calm, serene . . . whole.

"Where is the doctor?" he demanded of the bodyguard who sat in the living room.

"Across the hall, sir. In the lab," the man quickly replied.

The Kingpin walked into the best medical laboratory that money could buy. His wife's current doctor sat on a tall lab bench, reading a medical journal. It clattered to the table as he stood up.

"Mr. Fisk!"

"I've been visiting my wife in the solarium," the Kingpin said.

"Yes, sir. Mrs. Fisk seems to enjoy the sunlight—"

The Kingpin cut him off. "I sometimes have doubts that she even recognizes where she is. Obviously, she doesn't recognize me." He held out the crystal cameo. "She doesn't even recognize herself. Don't you allow Vanessa mirrors?"

"Why—of course, sir. Every morning as her hair is being styled, Mrs. Fisk sits in front of a large mirror—"

"Then why didn't she know this was her face?" The Kingpin's question came out as a shout.

His mood didn't improve as the doctor cringed even worse than Vanessa had.

The medical man looked like a whipped dog as he babbled something about the brain being a very delicate instrument.

"Listen, Doctor—" The Kingpin paused. He'd forgotten the doctor's name. There had been so many, over the years. "Is there nothing more that can be done for my wife?"

"I believe our present course of maintenance is the soundest medical treatment." Greasy sweat shone on the doctor's face. "We need to build up Mrs. Fisk. She was quite depressed by my predecessor's . . . accident."

The Kingpin's answer was a disgusted grunt.

He stood silently in the elevator taking him back to his office. One hand remained in his pocket, holding the cameo. The crystal was still warm against his fingers.

Once again, Aron Esterhazy's face appeared in his mind's eye. *The professor who had perfected himself.* Could his strange formula really be of help to Vanessa?

The Kingpin tried to keep current on the latest findings of science. Medical researchers had lately found that much of what been considered "mental illness" actually had a physical cause.

Could genetic perfection repair Vanessa's brain—perhaps restore her mind?

Spider-Man was ready to call "time out" on the Esterhazy search. On his own, he'd spent most of the last night swinging and looking. Now, with Daredevil, almost the whole day had gone by in a fruitless quest for the fugitive professor.

Daredevil had taken him on a tour of some of Manhattan's best hideouts. Those had to be the grungiest places he'd ever seen. There had been abandoned warehouses and hole-in-the-wall apartments, not to mention "hotels" not even roaches would live in.

It was enough to depress even a friendly, neighborhood Spider-Man.

And he still hadn't gotten away to Forest Hills. He'd called in twice. Mary Jane had said Aunt May's condition was the same. But there was no way that Spidey could leave off the search. Each phone call had been made with an impatient Daredevil lurking behind him.

Is this guy some kind of machine? Spider-Man grouchily wondered. *He keeps going, and going, and going—*

As evening came, Daredevil suggested that they knock off looking in ratholes and check the homeward-bound crowds. They'd swung over the student crunch leaving ESU, the commuter rush downtown, the crowds at the major train stations and bus depots.

While jam-packed with humanity, all had come up empty—of Dr. Esterhazy, that is. Several times along the way, they had come across traces of another search—the hunters sent out by the Kingpin. Even when thumping some of the street thugs, Spidey had taken heart to see them out and looking. It meant the bad guys still hadn't found Dr. Esterhazy.

Finally, Daredevil had made what Spider-Man considered the lamest suggestion yet. Spidey stood beside the red-clad hero atop a building overlooking Times Square.

"The theater crowd?" Spidey said in disbelief. "You really think Aron Esterhazy is hiding among the people going to the theaters? I don't think the guy ever watched anything except a test tube. He certainly never went to a Broadway show."

"I don't think he's going to see a play," Daredevil replied. "But the crowds at this time of night are perfect to hide someone going out to eat or get supplies." The handsome mouth under the red, horned mask gave him a tight smile. "Besides, we're next to the one remaining hideout area in Manhattan."

"Hell's Kitchen," Spider-Man said.

Daredevil nodded. "My stomping grounds."

"I wondered why we weren't checking around there," Spidey said.

"It would be easier to catch him in the streets," Daredevil replied.

"Right. Like he'd love to go for a walk down Broadway and maybe get himself a dirty-water hot dog—*hold it!*"

Spider-Man's attention had been caught by a figure moving through the crowd below. It was a tall man with white hair and a beaky nose. But he didn't walk with stooped shoulders like Dr. Esterhazy. Instead, he moved with the grace and power of a much younger man. What caught Spidey's eye, however, had been the clash between the man's white hair and the leather jacket he wore. The coat would have looked more at home on a young street punk.

"You see something?" Daredevil asked.

"Maybe. I think—" Spider-Man squinted, then his eyes went big. A faint buzzing sent a thrill through his nerves.

"Not maybe. My spider-sense is acting up. That must be our guy. Either that, or he's going to make some trouble for us."

They swung down to the sidewalk. As he came closer, Spider-Man was sure they were approaching Aron Esterhazy. But the weedy-looking professor was gone. This man was the ideal model of what Aron Esterhazy could be. His face had filled out, becoming more handsome. He was muscled like someone out of a comic book. And as he stepped up to confront the super heroes, Esterhazy seemed so ... *confident*.

"What is it now, Spider-Man?" the professor demanded.

Part of the crowd had begun to gawk and laugh at the costumed pair. "Must be a publicity stunt," someone said.

"I—ah—hey, lighten up, prof," Spider-Man said. "We've come here to help you."

"There were people from the government who used to say that," Esterhazy said. "The *money people* who got me into this whole problem were there to help me, too." His lips pulled back from his teeth in a feral snarl. "Why don't you just help me by going away? It seems that I can handle myself."

"Doctor, there are people after you," Daredevil began.

Esterhazy's humorless smile grew. "Where do you think I got this jacket? An overgrown lout tried to attack me. He didn't succeed."

"Doc, just because you beat a couple of street goons doesn't mean you can win out over the Kingpin," Spider-Man warned.

"Just let me be!" Esterhazy turned from them and began pushing his way through the crowd.

"Doctor, it doesn't go away that easily," Daredevil called after Esterhazy.

The professor began moving more quickly. In a few steps, he broke into a flat-out run. Daredevil found himself fighting through the crowd, falling behind.

"DD!" Spider-Man yelled. He aimed a web-shooter at a theater marquee and hoisted himself over the mob scene. "He's heading into the theater!"

People were just entering one of the theaters on Broadway. Esterhazy barreled his way through the gathering. He bowled over the ticket taker, and was inside.

Spider-Man came swinging down to the entrance, leaping high over the people clustered there. Daredevil was right behind him in three acrobatic leaps.

The interior of the theater was a madhouse, with people running around and screaming.

"Which way did he go?" Spider-Man shouted, his words lost in the crowd noise. Then he noticed some people picking themselves up from the stairs leading to the upper-level seats.

Daredevil had already scoped out the situation. Together, the heroes made a flying rush upstairs.

The higher they got, the more Spidey saw signs of Esterhazy's passage. A knot of ushers had been flattened at the entrance to the balcony. Spider-Man leapt over their stunned forms—and saw Esterhazy.

In his sleazy leather jacket, the professor stood out among the theatergoers. Spider-Man decided on the diplomatic approach. "Doctor Esterhazy, where do you think you're going?"

Esterhazy paid no attention. He headed for the side wall of the balcony, where racks of stage lights had been set up.

"Doc!" Spidey yelled.

The professor began scrambling up the pipe supports for the lights.

"I've been longer at this climbing business

than you have, Doc," Spider-Man muttered. "And my friend in red has even more hours logged than I do."

He sprang to the wall and began swarming up.

Esterhazy reached a catwalk up by the ceiling of the theater.

Daredevil flicked out his billy club, throwing a cable line that caught on the far end of the lighting platform. As he climbed up, he cut off Esterhazy's escape, while Spider-Man blocked the professor's retreat.

"Now, maybe we can talk about this calmly—" Spidey began.

But Esterhazy bounded off the metal pathway, launching himself toward a huge crystal chandelier that hung from the ceiling. The professor caught hold, and the chandelier swayed in a tinkle of glass as the crystals rattled together. Spidey saw a cable that stretched from the catwalk, holding the chandelier in place. Under the professor's weight, it snapped!

Cut loose, the chandelier went swooping toward the stage, crashing into and through the curtain.

"Well, that gives away the climax of the show," Spidey said.

Esterhazy dropped to the stage, apparently unhurt, and disappeared behind the curtain.

Spider-Man and Daredevil both swung down after him, but they'd lost precious seconds.

By the time they reached the stage door, Esterhazy was gone.

"At least we know where he is," Spider-Man said.

Daredevil nodded. "Yes. Somewhere in Hell's Kitchen."

Esterhazy bounded off the metal pathway, lauching himself toward a huge crystal chandelier that hung from the ceiling.

CHAPTER
—5—

News travels swiftly in the big city—especially news of interest to the Kingpin. The house manager of the theater quickly called the police about the break-in and spectacular escape. News went out from the nearest police precinct to reporters and to others with interest in what the police did. The news leaked from the city rooms of the newspapers. Tips also came from some of the theater goers who'd seen the unexpected show.

The result was that a lot of telephones began ringing in the Kingpin's office tower. And in a little while, the single phone on the big man's desk began to jangle.

"Yes?" This was an inside line, protected from tapping by every high-tech means possible. Even so, Wilson Fisk wasn't about to identify himself.

The voice on the other end of the line belonged to the rather battered lieutenant in charge of the search for Aron Esterhazy. "The target was spotted busting his way into a theater on Broadway. He was being chased by people we know. One climbs walls, and the other has horns."

"They subdued the object of our interest?" the Kingpin asked.

When he heard how Esterhazy had gotten away, his eyebrows rose—a sign of great surprise on his usual poker-face. "He escaped the pursuit of that pair? This may require rethinking our own plans."

He hung up, lost in thought. Judging from the reports coming in, this new, improved Esterhazy was already going through his street people like a hot knife through butter. If his defeated searchers were to be believed, Esterhazy had the strength of four normal men. Now it seemed he also had the agility and abilities to elude super heroes such as Spider-Man and Daredevil.

The Kingpin needed a much more powerful hunter. It had to be someone not only powerful, but expendable, considering his superpowered competition. Someone the Kingpin wouldn't mind seeing in jail. Someone who could be sacrificed—if necessary. Someone the Kingpin himself might have to turn on ... and eliminate.

A rare smile curved his heavy lips as he picked up his phone again. A second later, his lieutenant was on the line. "Get me the Hobgoblin," the Kingpin said. "And I have some special instructions on how he's to be treated."

"Nighttime in Hell's Kitchen," Spider-Man muttered to himself. "Another magical evening in the garden spot of New York City. What am I doing here?"

Behind his mask, he blinked his eyes. His lids felt as if someone had loaded them with sand while he wasn't looking.

Do blind eyes feel the same way when Daredevil gets tired? Spidey thought. The heroes had split up to cover more space. Spider-Man wondered if that hadn't been a mistake. Daredevil knew all the best places to hole up in this neighborhood. Spidey was just wandering the streets keeping an eye on things and poking around.

The super hero stifled a yawn. He shouldn't even be here. He'd been on this chase almost two days straight. Mary Jane wouldn't remember what he looked like. And Aunt May!

That's where he should be—out in Forest

Hills, seeing how his aunt was doing. Spidey thought of Dr. Esterhazy, about his strong new muscles, his sudden confidence. *If that genetic formula had done the old duffer so much good, what might it do for Aunt May?* Perhaps, when he caught up with the wandering professor, he could get a sample of the formula—

A muffled *thud* interrupted Spider-Man's thoughts. He was now near the Hudson River, swinging over a block of abandoned buildings. A subtle buzz in his brain warned him that something was up.

Almost lost in the shadows under a broken streetlight, two guys were trying to knock in the plywood that sealed one of the tenement doors. The big one was smashing with a sledgehammer. A smaller, pudgier figure heaved with a crowbar.

"We really gotta go lookin' in here, Turk?" Spidey heard a whining voice say. "That's no job for us!"

"You take the big guy's money, Grotto, you do what he wants," the big man, Turk, replied. "I'll hold the flashlight. You look."

"Oh, *man!*" Grotto complained.

With a crack like a pistol shot, the plywood broke. But before the pair could go in, Spider-Man was on them.

He flicked out a new line of webbing and

dropped on them from above. "Hey, guys," he said, "I think you're taking this house-breaking thing a bit too literally."

Scared eyes peered up at him from a pudding-like face. The other thug made a sound low in his throat and swung the sledge-hammer he was holding.

Spider-Man grabbed the head of the hammer, adding his weight to Turk's momentum. The goon lost his balance, staggered, then sprawled down the broken steps of the stoop.

"Ooh, that had to hurt." Spidey clung to the wall beside the doorway, turning to Grotto.

The second man stood rooted by the entrance. Bad smells came out of the opening. Grotto didn't want to go into the dark, stinking building. But he knew Spider-Man would be on his back if he tried to run. Finally, he tried to vault off the stoop, his hand darting under his short jacket.

"Bad choice," Spider-Man said.

Thwip! A strand of webbing grabbed at Turk's gun just as he pulled it free. Spider-Man yanked hard on the web-line, as if he were playing snap-the-whip. Caught in mid-air, the gunman crashed down onto the steps. He landed half across Turk, who groaned and *oofed*.

With a second snap, Spidey used his webbing to yank the gun right out of Grotto's nerveless fingers. Freeing it from the sticky strand, the hero tossed the gun into the lightless gloom of the tenement doorway. Rats scuttled as the pistol thumped on floorboards.

"So why does the Kingpin have you guys doing a house-to-house search in *this* neighborhood?" Spidey smacked his right fist into his open palm. "You *are* going to tell me, aren't you?"

From the sounds Grotto was making, he was having a hard time getting himself to breathe. Turk's surly voice finally replied. "Just orders, man. Everybody got the word to come here and start lookin'."

"Why?" Even as Spider-Man asked the question, he knew it was useless—these low-level punks wouldn't know.

"Forget about it, guys," he said. "My suggestion is that you call off the search. You never know what—or who—you might run into." Spider-Man fired off a web-line and swung over the flattened thugs. He had no time for rival hunters. He needed to find the quarry—and fast.

Moments later, a bat-winged, jet-powered platform swooped down out of the night sky over Hell's Kitchen. A human figure straddled the tiny flying machine, like a horseman rising in his stirrups. A hooded, vaguely medieval costume flapped in the breeze of his passage.

Then a shaft of moonlight glimmered on the face beneath the hood, revealing a nightmare vision. Its skin was scaly, and a sickly yellow color. The features were all wrong, too. Oversized, blazing red eyes flanked a pointed, drooping nose. Elf-like ears poked out of the cowled hood. The face tapered to a jaw that was too narrow to be human. The tight-lipped mouth above it was too huge— and displayed pointed fangs as the Hobgoblin snarled in annoyance.

Hell's Kitchen was an architectural hodgepodge, changing from block to block. Gaunt tenement buildings were being turned into luxury apartments for young executives. Old houses were being knocked down to make parking lots. Parking lots were being built up into new high-rises. And dead factories loomed in the darkness.

Somewhere down in those streets was a man he had to find and capture. More important right now, though, those streets should also hold some answers.

Hobgoblin was already aware of the Kingpin's Manhattan-wide search when he was called in. According to his sources, Aron Esterhazy had been working on some development of the old super-soldier formulas. Hobgoblin had even considered jumping into this search on his own. There were a lot of things he could do with perfected muscles and reflexes. For one thing, he could squash a certain spidery super hero like a bug.

He changed the course of his soaring jet when he spotted a pair of what could only be the Kingpin's men. They stood in front of a gutted tenement, arguing.

"—*gotta* come in with me, Turk," Hobgoblin heard an annoyed voice over his swooping jet. "The man threw my *gun* in there."

"Not me," Turk replied angrily. "I busted my flashlight tumbling down those stairs."

The pair didn't have time to say more. Hobgoblin came strafing down. A pumpkin bomb sent them tumbling for their lives.

As the Hobgoblin brought his jet-glider around, the hulking, darker thug clawed at his shoulder holster as he tried to scramble to his feet. Laughing, Hobgoblin shifted his weight on the jet. It flashed down, and the back of the petty criminal's coat caught on the jet-glider's horned figurehead.

Hobgoblin leaned back, taking the glider up, higher and higher. Turk's voice grew shrill as he kicked like a pinned bug. "Get off me!" He tried to pull his gun, but it seemed stuck in the holster.

The Hobgoblin flashed down, and the back of the petty crim-inal's coat caught on the jet-glider's horned figurehead.

"If I let you off, you'll fall," Hobgoblin said, mocking his prisoner. He set the glider to hover, then abruptly brought it down about a foot.

"Please!" his prisoner begged. "My coat— I can feel it giving!"

"Then tell me all you know about Esterhazy."

"I don't know much about the dude. King-pin says we all gotta find him, bring him in." Turk was almost gobbling as he told what little he knew. "And the spider, he's lookin', too. Me and my partner, we tangled with him."

"Interesting." Hobgoblin sent his little aircraft rocketing toward the ground. As they passed the pudgy figure who stared up at them open-mouthed, a blast-ray lashed from Hobgoblin's gauntlet. It split Turk's coat, freeing him from the horns—and plummeting him down on his partner. With a hideous laugh, the Hobgoblin wheeled his jet-glider around and headed off.

Launching himself into the darkness, Daredevil swung over the streets of Hell's Kitchen, scanning widely with his enhanced senses. The radar image of block after block came to him. He inhaled deeply, as if to track down the spoor of his quarry. Even over the perfumes and colognes of the theater audience, he'd detected the sharp, metallic tang of Aron Esterhazy's sweat.

But all this sensory input seemed to fade as the image of the professor's leap to safety blotted everything out. Nobody with poor eyesight could have tried that maneuver. Spider-Man's comment was accurate. The Esterhazy formula had improved the doctor's eyes.

Could it return sight to the sightless?

After his years in darkness, Matt Murdock had thought he'd come to accept his fate. He might be sightless, but he'd gotten other, powerful perceptions as compensation. He'd just about convinced himself that vision would only get in the way.

But the chance of holding a flower in his hand and *seeing* it, enjoying the visual beauty of the world—

From the streets below, two raucous voices swore at each other. Daredevil recognized them: a pair of the Kingpin's lowest-level enforcers, Turk and Grotto.

"It's jammed in here—broke!" Turk's furious voice burst out.

"Nearly broke my *neck,* fallin' on me like that!" Grotto squalled. "We don't know where this Easter-hoozy guy is, Spider-Man and Hobgoblin mess us up to find out where he is—" He gulped. "Man, can't we just go home?"

"Sure—if you want the Kingpin all over us, too," Turk replied.

The two beaten-up thugs tottered down the street, just about holding each other up.

Daredevil gave a wry smile as he swept off. For once, at least, he didn't have to *thump* the information out of them.

S omeone had taken a couple of shots at the streetlight. The lighting element hung swaying in the wind, flickering fitfully. It cast a circle of sickly radiance that moved back and forth, back and forth ... casting crazy shadows on the round-faced man standing on the street below.

For the hundredth time, he dug a scrap of paper from his coat pocket and looked at the address scribbled on it. The man's overcoat was expensive—far too good for the mean streets of Hell's Kitchen.

Dr. David Borloff tried to turn up his coat collar. He had to do it one-handed because of the large package he was carrying.

This blasted coat, he thought. *I might as well be wearing a big sign saying "rob me."*

Borloff scuttled along the street. The address he'd gotten over the phone was much farther west than he thought.

He seemed to be heading to the Hudson River. Streetlights became fewer, with farther distances between them. Even the sidewalks seemed to be crumbling away. The concrete was cracked and uneven. On some blocks, Borloff felt more like he was climbing stairs than walking along a street.

The chubby professor wasn't used to the exercise. After just a few blocks, he was breathing heavily and shifting his package from arm to arm.

Squinting along a line of abandoned tenements, Borloff unhappily sucked at his teeth. The doorways were either yawning holes, or they were boarded up. There didn't seem to be any doors. How could he tell the address he wanted?

Luckily, some building owner of the last century had carved the house number over his doorway. That must have been why this ruin of a building had been chosen for a meeting place.

David Borloff scuttled up the stoop and knocked.

The door opened a crack, then swung wide. "Come in—quickly! Did you bring all the items I asked for?"

Borloff stumbled after his mentor. He had always looked up to Aron Esterhazy. Now he gasped to find a man who seemed almost superhuman. Muscular arms whisked away his heavy package as if it weighed nothing.

But as Borloff looked more closely, he began taking note of certain inconsistencies. Frightening inconsistencies. Above Dr. Esterhazy's noble face, the front of his head seemed to be bulging unnaturally. The joints in his arms and legs fit together in an alien way.

Esterhazy didn't give his old pupil much time to inspect his physical development. With an almost rude grunt, the scientist turned his back on Borloff and led him deeper into the house. He jerked a thumb to a portable lantern hanging on the wall. "David, get that—"

His words were drowned out by a triumphant roar from outside. Something began crashing against the door.

Esterhazy turned in his tracks, his eyes blazing with fury. "You fool! They've followed you to reach me!"

"I—I didn't see anyone." Borloff tried to argue, but he was a scientist. He'd been taught to face facts.

From the number of rough voices beyond the door, there must have been an army out in the street. The wooden panel began to splinter.

Borloff glanced back, feeling a stab of panic. "Aron, what will we—"

He got no answer. And when he turned back, Borloff discovered that his revered teacher, his second father, had disappeared. As the door shattered, he was the only one standing in the flickering circle of lamplight.

Clinging to a dusty banister, David Borloff tried to back up a set of rickety stairs. He stared in terror as a mob of the cruelest, ugliest, meanest-looking men he'd ever seen in his life advanced on him.

"Where is he?" demanded a totally hairless guy with a huge scar across his face.

He stepped forward, a knife that looked more like a sword gleaming in his large, hairy hand. "Yo, wimp, I'm talking to—"

His threat was lost in a new outburst of yelling from outside. Howls of victory were turning into cries of pain and fury.

The scarred thug with the big knife turned as his comrades seemed to explode inward from the doorway. Spider-Man burst through the opening to confront the knife-wielder. Shouting "Coming through!", the hero bounced over the thug as if he were playing leap-frog.

The enraged goon slashed upward, but

Spider-Man was already past him. The scarred hoodlum twisted round for another go—only to crash right into the hero's fist.

Scarface went down like a poleaxed steer. This battle had ended quickly, but the war was far from over.

About five hundred of the thug's friends came charging up for revenge. Spider-Man wasn't just tackled, he was buried under his attackers.

"Gotcha, freak!" shouted one of the hoodlums.

Then he and his fellow goons went flying as if a land mine had exploded beneath them. Spider-Man was back on his feet, ready to meet the next rush through the door.

A bloodthirsty crowd jammed the doorway. Then Borloff heard more screeching and shouting from outside, and Daredevil rocketed in—right over the heads of the mass of thugs blocking the entrance.

"Thought I'd find you in here," Daredevil said, hurling some of the flattened hoods into the mass of attackers.

"Yeah, that crowd in the street was a dead giveaway," Spider-Man said. As he spoke, his left fist connected with three jaws in quick succession. His right wrist threw webbing over another half-dozen of Hell's Kitchen's fiercest street thugs.

Daredevil was using his billy club to great effect as well. The mass of goons was no longer madly charging at the super heroes. There were too many bodies of their buddies lying around for any charging to be done.

The horned hero glanced at the quivering Borloff, and shouted to Spider-Man: "I'm afraid your new friend might get in the way while we finish up with these characters."

"I'll handle it!" Spider-Man vaulted up to the head of the stairs.

As Borloff turned to see what he was up to, he heard a *thwip!* as something hit him in the chest. Then he was suddenly soaring through the air, yanked on a thick line of webbing.

It was too much for the researcher. With a sigh, his head fell forward ... and he passed out.

High over a block of ruined tenements, Hobgoblin circled on his jet-glider. The scene below looked like the old horror film where a mob of villagers tries to get the monster.

Only in this movie, the villagers were attacked from behind by a second monster.

Hobgoblin smiled as he watched Daredevil fight his way to the door. Good. Now all the hunters were in one place ...

A lone figure suddenly appeared on the roof

He and his fellow goons went flying as if a land mine had
exploded beneath them. Spider-Man was back on his feet.

of the building where the war was going on. Hobgoblin got a glimpse of white hair, and flew his jet-glider up out of earshot. His plan had worked. The gathering of hunters had flushed out his prey.

At long range, he followed Aron Esterhazy as the professor fled across the rooftops. The old tenements were packed so closely together that from a distance they seemed to be one giant building, taking up most of the block. Then there was a fifteen-foot gap where one of the tenements, more rotted away than the others, had been knocked down.

The space between roofs was bridged by a single wooden board. Still carrying his package, Esterhazy climbed onto this wobbly connection and started across. Hobgoblin was impressed. The professor must have absolute confidence in his perfected muscles and balance.

The villain decided to hold off on swooping down. He might catch his prey in a helpless position. But he might accidentally knock Esterhazy off the board sixty feet above the ground. The professor had to live—because Hobgoblin was determined to steal the perfection formula.

Down below, the professor had reached the far roof. He was almost a full block away now from the fighting down the street. Esterhazy crossed to the rooftop door of an odd-shaped little penthouse. He opened the door and started down the stairs inside.

Hobgoblin circled the building for a moment or two, giving Esterhazy a chance to reach ground level. The scientist didn't emerge. *So this must be his hide-out,* the villain realized.

Throttling down his jet-glider, Hobgoblin landed on the roof. Entering through the same door, he searched his way down through the building, checking each floor. There was no sign of Esterhazy until Hobgoblin reached the basement.

The windowless room shimmered with the light of a dozen candles and a couple of kerosene lamps. His face pinched with concentration, Aron Esterhazy held up a test tube in the flickering glow. Again, Hobgoblin had guessed correctly. The package contained not food or clothing, but the ingredients for Esterhazy's formula. The professor was continuing his research.

Hobgoblin waited till Esterhazy was finished. Then he threw a couple of goblin mini-bombs. The small explosives weren't enough to cause much damage—but they blew out most of the lights in the room and knocked the surprised scientist off his feet. Throttling up his jet-glider, Hobgoblin *whoosh*ed across the room to confront Esterhazy. But he didn't try to capture the astonished scientist.

Instead, the villain snatched a plugged test-tube from Esterhazy's hand. In the feeble gleam of a surviving kerosene lamp, Hobgoblin's misshapen mask was twisted in a mocking smile.

"A fair trade, Doctor," he said. "Your freedom for your formula."

His laughter died as a new voice suddenly cut in.

"No deal, Hobgoblin."

The villain whirled around on his jet-glider, his face now a mixture of fury and surprise.

Standing at the entrance to the stairs was the last person on Earth he expected to see.

"Spider-Man!"

Over the years, the wall-crawler had often turned up in just the wrong place at the right time, ruining Hobgoblin's plans and causing him to flee. This appearance, though, was a particularly nasty surprise.

The hero was blocking the only exit from the room!

Spider-Man took another step into the darkened space, treading easily but keeping a watchful eye on the Hobgoblin. "I left Daredevil to deal with the assistant baddies, and took off after the professor," he said. "Fortunately, I noticed *you* zooming after him, too."

The hero glanced over at Esterhazy. "Well, Doc," he said, "maybe now you see why you need help. Our friend the Kingpin has brought in his varsity team to deal with you."

"The vial," Esterhazy said, his voice sounding numb with shock. "That creature has my formula!"

The news stopped Spider-Man in his tracks. He froze, his head whipping round like a targeting device to stare at the stoppered test-tube the Hobgoblin held. If the Kingpin got his hands on the formula, it would be a disaster. He would create an army of superpowered goons. And he would no longer have a reason to take Aron Esterhazy alive. Indeed, he would want the professor dead to ensure that no one else ever got hold of the formula.

Spider-Man slowly advanced on his old enemy, wagging a taunting finger. "Naughty-naughty, Hobbsy," he scolded. "That formula doesn't belong to you—or to the Kingpin."

If I can get close enough to jump at him, he thought, *maybe I can wrestle the vial away.*

Hobgoblin's laughter returned, louder than ever. "You think I would give this prize to *that* overweight idiot?" he sneered. "The perfection formula is far more valuable—to me! I'll study it, then use it on myself. And after perfecting myself, I'm going to crush you like the insect you are!"

Spider-Man tensed for a leap as the Hobgoblin made his move—but it wasn't toward the stairway that Spidey blocked.

With a sudden roar, Hobgoblin's jet-glider streaked toward a huge square of plywood set in the wall beyond Esterhazy. The wooden barrier splintered, revealing a dark shaftway.

"A dumbwaiter!" Spider-Man cried in dismay. Some old buildings had dumbwaiters, a sort of hand-operated elevator for hoisting packages between floors. Often the dangerous old shaftways had been boarded up. By smashing through that panel, Hobgoblin had given himself a free route right up to the roof!

Got to stop him, Spidey thought, dashing for the irregular opening his enemy had torn through the plywood. Just as he arrived, he saw an orange shape come bouncing down out of the darkness. The Hobgoblin had left a goodbye present—a pumpkin bomb!

Thwip! With a desperate flick, Spider-Man fired his webbing to englobe the bomb.

It went off with a muffled *fwooomf!*", the worst of its blast contained by the webbing. The super hero staggered back in the shock wave. But in an instant he lurched forward again, firing a line of webbing up into the dark shaft. Soon he was climbing up after the Hobgoblin.

A sudden crash from above showed that Hobgoblin had reached the top of the dumbwaiter shaft—and torn through the roof.

Spidey dodged the debris that tumbled down. He emerged into the night to find a triumphant Hobgoblin swooping high into the sky, ready to escape.

"Not so fast!" a new voice cried. Daredevil raced across the roof on the other side of the demolished building. Leaping into the air, he brought back his arm and whipped his billy club around. The curved handle of the club flashed upward, trailing a cable.

It was a tricky throw, but Daredevil managed it perfectly. The weighted line whipped around the right-hand wing of Hobgoblin's jet-glider, holding tight. Daredevil had lassoed the flying platform!

Hobgoblin's jet-glider wobbled under the new weight, losing altitude even as he sped on. Daredevil swung along at the end of his cable like a human yo-yo.

Time for me to get into the game, Spider-Man thought, firing a web-line to the water tower on a building across the street.

"Now to do that Tarzan thing," he said, swinging out to confront Hobgoblin.

There was no way the villain couldn't see him coming. And there was no place for Spider-Man to hide from his weapons. Apparently, Hobgoblin considered Spidey the more dangerous of the two heroes zeroing in on him. He lobbed a pumpkin bomb at the wall-crawler, trying to keep him away.

Slewing around at the end of his web-line, Spider-Man changed course and avoided the blast.

"You ought to brush up a little more on the old pitching," he advised the flying villain. "Practice makes perfect. Maybe you can hang a tire in your hide-out, see if you can get a bomb through the middle without touching—"

"Mock me while you can, insect," Hobgoblin growled.

"How many times do I have to tell you criminal types?" Spider-Man teased. "Spiders aren't insects. They're—whoops!"

The Hobgoblin had launched another pumpkin bomb. Spider-Man could see its little jack-o-lantern face gleaming as it flew right toward his chest.

Hurling his weight to the right, Spider-Man dodged past the deadly little toy. He braced himself against the blast as the bomb went off behind him. Here was where the tide turned. Now he was in webbing range.

Thwip! his web-shooter fired a line of gooey webbing that caught Hobgoblin square in the chest.

"Gotcha now, Hobbsy," Spidey said. "Why don't you make this easier on all of us and give up?"

Still holding the vial of perfection formula in one hand, Hobgoblin dug out another pumpkin bomb. The jet-glider wobbled, unbalanced by the tug of Daredevil, who was still attached to the craft by his billy club cable.

Hobgoblin tossed the glowing bomb underhand. It seemed to move in slow motion, and Spider-Man had no trouble avoiding the glowing orange sphere.

"Come on, Hobbsy," he said. "Your aim's supposed to get better as I come closer."

"Oh, I aimed that one . . . *perfectly!*" Hobgoblin snarled. He twisted on his jet-glider, streaking in an aerial U-turn until he was right over the bomb. Spider-Man spun round, caught in a game of snap-the-whip.

The pumpkin bomb went off, its blast making the jet-platform reel through the air.

Then Spider-Man realized what Hobgoblin had done. The bomb hadn't been meant for him. Hobgoblin's real target was the cable wrapped around the right wing of his glider—the cable that connected with Daredevil's billy club. It was the horned hero's lifeline, which the bomb-blast had just severed!

Daredevil was in free fall. Five stories of empty air lay between him and the hard, cold ground.

"It's your choice, Spider-freak," Hobgoblin cackled. "You can save your friend, or you can capture me."

"He's not my friend," Spider-Man objected. But even as he spoke, he released the web-line that connected him to Hobgoblin.

Spidey stretched out his arms almost in opposite directions. *Thwip! Thwip!* Web-strands shot out from both of the hero's wrists.

Got to aim this just right, he thought.

One target was hard to miss—the wall of a building above him. His more difficult shot caught Daredevil in the back. Heaving against both web-lines, Spider-Man broke his fellow hero's fall.

He landed against the wall, steadying himself as he let Daredevil down to the ground. Even as he worked, he scanned the sky for the Hobgoblin's jet-glider.

The flying platform had taken some damage from the bomb-blast. Part of the right wing was torn and crumpled. But the Hobgoblin was still airborne—and he was far out of reach.

Spider-Man's old enemy knew he was safe. He turned back as he crouched over his jet-glider, holding up the tube he still held.

"I've got Esterhazy's formula! See you soon, Spider-Man." A tone of menace crept into Hobgoblin's jeering. "Just as soon as I've tasted perfection, I'll come and finish with you."

But he should have kept his eyes on his driving.

Hobgoblin aimed to jet off over a loft building that was flanked by two taller factories. Suddenly, a metal pipe peeled off the side of one of the taller structures.

Spider-Man blinked. It was one of the drainpipes that snaked down along the walls of dirty brick. Slowly, almost lazily, the tin pipe swung downward. Its fall perfectly intersected with Hobgoblin's course.

Laughing wildly, the vial of Esterhazy's formula still held over his head, Hobgoblin turned from his taunting and faced front.

The falling pipe caught him squarely across the chest. It was as though he'd run into a tripwire. The damaged jet-glider bucked and wobbled under the super-villain's feet. The magno-lock stirrups holding him in place failed. The jetting platform flew on. But the Hobgoblin did not.

For a second, it looked as though he'd wrap himself around the pipe that had clotheslined him. Instead, he bounced off.

Hobgoblin arced backward, two legs and one arm flailing. His other arm clutched the vial of perfection formula protectively to his chest.

The roof of the loft building was perhaps a dozen feet below the villain. Even Spider-Man winced at the noise of Hobgoblin's impact.

"Now, that's *got* to leave a mark," the hero said.

The vial of Esterhazy's formula still held over his head, Hob-goblin turned from his taunting and faced front.

The unpiloted jet-glider wobbled on for a second or two more. Then it crashed into another abandoned building, going up with a roar.

As the fireworks cleared away, human voices caught the hero's attention. He'd been concentrating just on the Hobgoblin, but now he saw activity on the roof of the building where the villain had fallen. Ropes were dropping from the cornice of the roof. Men began to descend the dingy brick wall, rappelling their way down commando-style.

The door on the stairway penthouse banged open, and more men poured out of the stairs. Some wore expensive-looking suits. Others were in camouflage combat suits, like the men swarming down the ropes.

All carried big guns.

It would be nice to think that the boys in blue would respond quickly to the sort of riot we've been causing, Spider-Man thought. *But somehow, I don't think those guys are the cops.*

His suspicions were justified a moment later, when the last man came out onto the roof. He was a big, stocky guy, and he didn't carry a gun. Instead, he swaggered over to the fallen Hobgoblin, his hands in his pockets.

What really struck Spider-Man, however,

was the man's sneering, hard, somewhat bruised face. He recognized the guy.

It was the same man who'd visited Aron Esterhazy to threaten him and collect the formula. The man who—however unintentionally —had helped transform the professor into his present superhuman state.

CHAPTER

—8—

The world was hazy for the Hobgoblin as he opened his eyes. But the fog quickly faded away. He could make out the night sky above him.

Then he noticed a gun muzzle. And another. And another.

Hobgoblin stopped counting the guns covering him as he remembered how he'd wound up here. His hand jerked. Yes, the tube of perfection formula had come through unharmed.

His sudden movement brought a chorus of *click*s from the weapons trained on him. The villain froze. The grim faces on the men behind the guns looked just as hard as the weapons they held.

Another face appeared over him, one he

recognized. Those tough, bruised features belonged to the man who had hired him—a lieutenant of the Kingpin.

"So this is Esterhazy's formula, huh?" The hard man reached for the test tube.

Hobgoblin's hand clenched defensively around his prize.

A gun was suddenly pressed to his forehead. He could feel the cold metal of the muzzle even through the plastex of his mask.

"You wouldn't be thinking of holding out on us," the boss thug said. "Would you, Hobgoblin? I mean, a guy might get the wrong idea from some of the stuff you were yelling at Spider-Man. But I figure that was just excitement talking. A smart guy like you wouldn't try double-crossing the Kingpin."

He stretched out a relentless hand. "Now, give."

Wordlessly, Hobgoblin raised the stoppered test tube and passed it over. The only sound he heard was the grinding of his teeth.

Then something else came to his ears—the rhythmic, almost twittering roar of a helicopter engine. As he thought about it, Hobgoblin realized he'd been hearing a chopper engine throughout the evening. It must have been circling all during his fight—which meant this treacherous stooge had been following him all through his hunt.

Hobgoblin's mouth was brassy with pent-up rage. He wanted to leap to his feet, blast the man with the formula, retrieve it—

But he didn't dare. Too many guns were still trained on him.

The Kingpin's lieutenant must have caught some hint to his thoughts.

"You just take it easy, pal. We'll get this to the boss." He smiled without a trace of humor. "It could have been worse. If I had to, I was supposed to take this over your dead body."

A small helicopter landed on the roof, and the head thug got in. The little force of gunmen also boarded, their guns aimed constantly at the Hobgoblin.

With a groan, the Hobgoblin sat up, glaring after the dwindling aircraft. The world went out of focus, swimming around him.

Groaning again, he sank back on the roof-top. His jet-glider was gone. There was no way he could follow. And, for the moment at least, all the fight had been knocked out of him.

Two other figures followed the path of the disappearing helicopter. One stared after it. The other followed its course with a radar sense.

"Hobgoblin got a sample of the formula from Esterhazy," Spider-Man said.

"And soon it will be in the Kingpin's hands," Daredevil finished. "I'd say that chopper is headed directly for the big guy's office tower."

"Then that's where we ought to go," Spidey said. "This isn't over yet."

For the few people who happened to be looking skyward, the two heroes put on a thrilling aerial show as they hurtled their way uptown.

The Kingpin's white office tower jutted up arrogantly into the night sky, a monument to his power and greed. Both heroes knew that the soaring structure was also a fortress—they had each tangled with its security systems often enough.

"So which do you think is the best way in?" Spider-Man asked.

"I usually go in through one of the windows," Daredevil answered.

"And I usually tackle this joint from the roof," Spidey said.

"The easiest way up is the big blank wall," Daredevil added.

Spider-Man nodded. "It won't be so easy without your billy club." He began fashioning a sort of harness out of webbing.

"What's that?"

"It's your ride. I think I can take you up the wall piggy-back."

Perhaps its was undignified, but it worked. The pair of heroes reached the rooftop without a problem.

"Whoof," Spider-Man muttered. "I know folks call me the wall-crawler, but when you do it for *that* many floors—"

"The helicopter has been here and gone," Daredevil interrupted. He inhaled deeply. "But not too long ago. I can still smell the exhaust of the aviation fuel."

"You think the Kingpin hopped aboard?"

"That would be the safe way," Daredevil admitted. "But it wouldn't be the Kingpin's way. Big Willie Fisk would never want anyone to think that he ran. I'm betting he's still inside."

Spidey nodded. "Then let's pay him a visit."

Boldly, they stepped onto the roof, ignoring the security cameras. On other visits, they would have tried for stealth, to creep past the Kingpin's defenses. But now there wasn't time.

A sudden buzz shrilled in Spider-Man's head. "Danger!" he announced.

"Machinery activating—over there!" Speaking at almost the same time, Daredevil pointed to the right.

They were already in motion as the automated blast-weapon swung up out of the roof and tried to target them. Spider-Man ripped the heavy weapon right off its mountings. Then they used the exposed gun-pit as their entrance into the building, even as other automated defenses covered the roof with blazing fire.

Insdie the building, Spider-Man's built-in danger warnings and the input of Daredevil's marvelous senses helped them avoid a gas attack and a hallway booby-trapped to electrocute them. The goon squad that came charging upstairs was easily handled as well. Spider-Man went low, webbing the guards' feet together. Daredevil went high, bouncing off the ceiling to land feet-first in the tangled pile.

In seconds, the thugs were disarmed, unconscious, or both.

"You know, those alarm bells are beginning to get on my nerves," Spider-Man complained.

"If you think *you* have it bad, think how it sounds to someone with super-sensitive hearing," Daredevil replied with a grin.

They bypassed another corridor whose ceiling was rigged to fall on whoever came through. "This is a new one," Spider-Man said.

Daredevil wasn't impressed. "Sort of like the trap where the walls are built to squish you together."

They faced another security squad, this one armed with grenades. A hastily webbed shield provided protection from the blasts. There was no one to protect the bad guys, however, when the heroes got too close for bomb range.

"Well, that pretty much blew up this office," Spider-Man said.

"Fisk usually doesn't allow explosives inside the building," Daredevil said.

Spidey shrugged. "Maybe he's going to redecorate. Anyway, I think we set a new record for getting in to see Fatso."

"Where do we look for him?" Daredevil asked. "His gym or his office?"

"The office," Spider-Man replied. "I'd hate to mess up the man's gym."

In front of the executive offices they found a pale, unhappy looking leg-breaker sitting at the secretary's desk.

"The Boss—er, Mr. Fisk—said he's waiting for you in the solarium." His face seemed to beg *please don't kill me*.

"Two floors up, on the east side?" Spider-Man asked.

The thug nodded, obviously glad he didn't have to guide them.

"You just stay right here. And, to make sure you don't touch any security doohickeys—" Two quick jets of webbing glued the man's hands to the desktop.

"Don't worry," Spidey assured the thug, who was unsuccessfully trying to free himself. "The webbing dissolves in a couple of hours."

The floor devoted to Vanessa Fisk's quarters was empty when the heroes arrived. They went into the solarium on guard for some sort of trap. Spider-Man expected to find the place jammed with bazooka-wielding ninjas.

Instead, they found four people. The Kingpin sat in a specially made chair. Beside him was an older woman who looked vaguely familiar. The Kingpin's wife, Vanessa, lay in a long lounger. Beside her stood a doctor in a lab coat.

"Gentlemen," the Kingpin said expansively, as if he were used to greeting people who had stormed their way into his presence. "May I present Mrs. Elise Esterhazy," he said, nodding toward the woman who stood beside him. "We're about to test her husband's formula."

To put it mildly, Mrs. Esterhazy was scared green. "You!" she cried, staring at Spider-Man.

From beneath his mask, Spider-Man stared back. Recognition finally came. This was the woman he'd saved from the two muggers a couple of nights ago!

Or *had* they been muggers? One of them had claimed a connection with the Kingpin, although Spidey had laughed it off. He realized that the "mugging" had probably been a kidnapping, an attempt by the crime boss to gain leverage on Esterhazy.

"If you've touched her—" Spider-Man warned, perfectly willing to wade into battle.

"Mrs. Esterhazy is my guest," the Kingpin replied blandly. "Isn't that right, dear lady?"

Elise Esterhazy managed a nod and a squeaked "Yes."

"You kidnapped her and she's scared spitless of you!" Spider-Man accused.

"How very moral, for a costumed vigilante who has just smashed his way into my home," the Kingpin replied. "I merely offered Mrs. Esterhazy my protection. Her husband has apparently turned into a one-man crime wave, getting into fights all over Manhattan."

Spider-Man's fingers clenched into a fist. How pleasant it would feel to smash that arrogant face!

"You mean he's been fighting your goon squads, who were all out looking for him. We saw them at work in Hell's Kitchen, smashing places, hassling people—"

The Kingpin's eyebrows rose. "What have

I to do with the activities of street criminals? I'm a legitimate businessman. Import-export. A bit of medical research . . ."

"Funny how you run that research, threatening a scientist's life," Spider-Man said sarcastically.

"Are we referring to the scientist who *illegally* ran off with the results of his research, breaking a legal contract? A man who mixed up a sample of the formula, apparently, for a super-powered menace? I should think you'd be glad that my security people managed to recover my property—" the Kingpin allowed himself a little smile "—before it was put to evil use."

Spidey's throat was as tightly clenched as his fists. Of course. Fat Boy Fisk looked a hundred percent legal. At least, he had a hundred percent deniability. From the look on Daredevil's face, there was no doubt that the Kingpin had the law, if not justice, on his side.

The physician reached into a white ceramic container sitting on a table beside Vanessa Fisk. There was a clatter as his nervous fingers picked up a hypodermic syringe.

"Is that the formula?" Spider-Man barked. "Put that down!"

The doctor nearly dropped the hypo as the Kingpin stepped in front of the two super heroes. He had enough bulk for four people, and the fighting skills to challenge Spider-Man and Daredevil together. But there was an odd light in his eyes as he glanced from one hero to the other.

"I would just like to point out that it seems—unlikely—that Dr. Esterhazy will ever provide me with another sample of his research," he said. "I have elected to use this single sample as treatment . . . for my *wife*."

Spidey and Daredevil looked at each other in bafflement. The big guy was bargaining with them! If they agreed not to intervene, he would use the only sample of the perfection formula to cure his wife!

For a second, Spider-Man almost shouted "No! I have a sick aunt who could use that shot just as much as Vanessa Fisk!"

Beside him, Daredevil seemed to be waging an internal struggle as well. Finally, the red-clad hero said, "I suppose we could all think of good persons or places where that sample could be used. But it was developed with your money. I'm surprised to see you use it so— altruistically."

Spidey nodded. It was a surprise to see anything that fell into Wilson Fisk's hands being used in the cause of good.

"I'm hardly altruistic," the Kingpin said,

turning to his wife. His gaze seemed to eat her up. "This is something *I* want, very much."

He nodded to the doctor, who raised Vanessa Fisk's right sleeve, dabbed at her arm with alcohol, and found a vein. Frowning with concentration, he raised the needle—

—Just as an urgent buzzing filled Spider-Man's head.

If this is such a good thing, he wondered, *why is my spider-sense screaming danger?*

CHAPTER
—9—

The answer to Spider-Man's question came as the building alarms, which had finally quieted, began wailing again. Everyone in the room froze, uncertain of what would happen next.

Even through the soundproof glass, they could hear the discharge of energy weapons being fired outside. An intercom immediately burst into life. "Mr. Fisk! Sir! We've got another intruder! Unknown flying object—"

Then the glass wall of the solarium exploded inward, filling the air with glass shards. It was like standing in a deadly hailstorm.

The doctor was nearest to the window. He staggered and yelled in pain as razor-sharp fragments struck him.

x

101

Spider-Man couldn't help the man. In fact, despite the warnings of his spider-sense, he took several nasty nicks as he ducked and twisted. He hardly noticed the cuts as he fought to get Mrs. Esterhazy safely behind the cover of a chair that had tipped over.

The Kingpin grabbed Vanessa from her lounger. He held her to him as he knelt, sheltering her with his body. Jagged bits of glass sleeted past the crime boss. His spotlessly white, hand-tailored suit was ragged and splotched with startling red blots of blood by the time it was over.

"—a missile?" Elise Esterhazy cried from behind the chair where she crouched. Spidey could barely hear her over the jangling of danger warnings.

Spider-Man scanned the room frantically, the buzzing inside his head warning that he had missed something in all the confusion.

Now he realized that there was someone else in the room, and that the destruction hadn't come from a weapon blast. The huge glass panel had been smashed in by a jet-glider—a new one, judging from the looks of it as it went into hover mode over the fallen doctor.

And standing astride the flying platform was the same old Hobgoblin.

The villain also had the same problems on

his mind. "You fat fool!" he shrieked at the Kingpin. "Were you really going to waste perfection on poor little wifey? I think not! That formula is *mine*—so don't any of you get in my way!"

Hobgoblin's inhuman red eyes glowed with the fires of madness as he gazed around the suddenly still room.

Beneath the villain, the doctor groaned from where he lay sprawled out. He glanced dazedly around. Blood from a cut on his forehead ran down into his face. He didn't seem to realize what was going on.

But when he reached for the hypodermic he'd dropped, Hobgoblin flashed into movement. Thrusting out his arm, he discharged what seemed to be a bolt of fireworks into the physician's face.

Screaming, the medical man rolled on the floor, trying to smother a dozen small fires in his clothing.

The jet-glider *whoosh*ed forward barely an inch over the prone man's head. Hobgoblin seemed to see nothing else in the room as he snatched up the needle.

He whirled the platform around, lining up for a run to ram the Kingpin aside and grab Vanessa Fisk as a hostage.

Moving with incredible speed for a man of his bulk, the Kingpin beat Hobgoblin's move toward his wife. Roughly, he shoved Vanessa behind him, his teeth gritting at her whimpers of fear.

But he made it. He was between danger and his wife. And, from the look on Wilson Fisk's face, the Hobgoblin had just made a potentially fatal career move.

The Hobgoblin clearly couldn't care less as he jetted straight into the big man.

Ducking under the jet-glider with a new burst of unexpected agility, the Kingpin heaved upward. He managed to shove the platform off course.

But the Kingpin paid for his victory. Spider-Man could hear the flesh of his hands sizzle against the heat of the jet engine's cowling.

At least the big man had the reward of Hobgoblin's yell of surprise. The villain danced against his control-stirrups, fighting to redirect the sudden lift before he smeared himself against the painted ceiling.

Gotta get him off that thing, Spidey thought as he skidded across the floor. He came in under the Hobgoblin, firing upward with both web-shooters to hit the belly of the jet.

Working with incredible speed, he webbed the flying platform to the solid marble floor, draining one of his web-shooters in the process. *If this thing holds, it may do the trick!*

The webbing stretched to its maximum length, then snapped back like a giant rubber band.

The Hobgoblin's flier was snatched out of the air to crash nose-first into the floor.

Somehow, Hobgoblin managed to free his feet from the glider's stirrups. He leapt away from his useless vehicle, the hypodermic needle still in his hand. His other hand swept around to aim a blast-bolt at Spider-Man. But before Hobgoblin could fire, he was rammed in midair by a hurtling body.

Daredevil had entered the fray.

Hobgoblin fought like a mad dog, viciously determined to tear free. He didn't care what weapons he used in the confined space of the solarium. His blinding flash-weapon didn't faze Daredevil. But the razor-tipped homing bats he tossed into the air had everyone in the room ducking.

Furniture was smashed with blast-rays, or blown to bits by pumpkin bombs.

Spider-Man took on the job of fielding those deadly little packages, knocking them outside where they wouldn't do any harm. There were no windows left by this point, so he had a clear field for his anti-bombing exercises.

"Like playing handball with hand grenades," he muttered, smacking a jack-o-lantern off into space. It exploded into a fat, flaming mass.

"Yow! An incendiary bomb! Enough is enough!" Spider-Man waded in, changing the struggle to hand-to-hand combat.

Hobgoblin had stashed the hypo somewhere and was slugging wildly with both hands. He tried to hurl Daredevil out the window, but the Man Without Fear spun away to land safely. Then Spider-Man went toe-to-toe with the villain, slamming blows back and forth.

"I—aah!—can take more of—oof!—this than you can," Spidey panted. It was true. He could unleash three piston-like punches to Hobgoblin's two.

It seemed to last forever, but finally the villain went down.

Spider-Man leapt to finish him, only to get both of Hobgoblin's feet smashing into his stomach. His overloaded spider-sense had given him warning an instant too late. And why was it still buzzing in his head?

Spider-Man found out as he crashed into Daredevil, who was charging back into the battle.

The two of them went down as the intruder alarms began a new round of wailing. The sound of gunshots echoed from below through the now-empty windows. As the heroes tensed for another rush at their adversary, a heavy pounding threatened to splinter the solarium's still-locked door.

The Hobgoblin was back on his feet, his chest heaving as he faced everyone in the room. "Your hounds are scratching at the door, fat man," he said mockingly. "But they don't frighten me."

"No? Well, I bet you'll probably scare them," Spider-Man said. "You look like something out of a bad slasher flick."

None of them looked very pleasant. But that was to be expected of anyone who survived a war zone. And the solarium had been turned into exactly that.

Not a stick of furniture remained—it was scattered in pieces across the floor. The doctor lay unconscious, bloody and singed. Vanessa Fisk was physically unharmed, but in complete mental collapse, curled up in a little ball. The Kingpin stood bestride her. He had split the back of his bloody jacket, and his hands were red and blistering. Elise Esterhazy hadn't been hit by anything, but the elderly woman was crouched in terror.

And both Daredevil and myself will have to retire these costumes after this fight, Spider-Man thought. *They're too torn up to use as anything but cleaning rags.*

Besides the nicks and rips in his link-armor,

the Hobgoblin's costume had been completely torn off one shoulder. It gave Spidey an eerie feeling to see where the yellow skin of the villain's mask gave way to the pink tones of healthy flesh.

The thunder against the door intensified.

"Bring them on!" Hobgoblin cried. "I'll be ready for them!"

He raised his arm. Spider-Man gasped. Somehow, the villain had managed to come up with the hypodermic filled with Esterhazy's formula.

"Perfection will be mine," Hobgoblin brayed. "If this stuff works the way I've heard, I should have the strength to defeat both Spider-Man *and* Daredevil. Then I'll handle your pitiful forces—and take care of you."

Wilson Fisk stood with his arms ready to swing. His head was down and forward, making him look like a bull preparing to charge. The usual cold disdain in his eyes was gone, replaced with blood-lust.

"And if it doesn't work as you expect?" The Kingpin's voice was deep and guttural as he spoke. Spider-Man realized the huge man was moments away from blowing up completely.

Hobgoblin answered with a mad, jangling

laugh. "It won't matter. The formula will still be *mine!*"

He held the hypodermic as if it were a knife, ready to stab it into his arm.

Spider-Man and Daredevil were back on their feet, tensed for another rush. This fight was no longer about saving the formula for Vanessa Fisk. It would be a struggle to keep the formula out of Hobgoblin's bloodstream. If the hypo got destroyed in the battle, so be it.

Although, Spidey had to admit, he wasn't exactly sure how the Kingpin would react to that result.

Hobgoblin brought the needle plunging down on his bared flesh, just as—

—The hinges of the door finally gave way with a painful screech of tortured metal.

The heavy portal crashed down on Hobgoblin before he could inject himself. He twisted around to face the intruder and stared.

Elise Esterhazy looked up into the doorway and screamed.

The pounder on the door was definitely *not* a detachment of the Kingpin's guards.

"*Four* break-ins in a row," Spider-Man muttered. "Boy, building security is taking a beating tonight!"

CHAPTER
—10—

The apparition in the doorway was so nightmarish, it made Hobgoblin look normal and homey. A huge, hulking monster leaned against the twisted and broken door frame, panting for breath.

Nothing about the creature seemed to match. One huge arm was covered in grayish fur. The other had a lizard's scales and claws. The left leg would have looked more at home on a giant chicken. The right leg seemed human, encased in the tatters of a pair of pants. It even wore a shoe.

"What is this?" Spider-Man demanded, "an escapee from your labs? The amazing four-way man? Kingpin, you've been involved in some pretty ugly business, but this—"

"It's none of my doing," the Kingpin hissed.

If someone knew what to look for, Spidey realized, he might be able to recognize the remains of Aron Esterhazy in this creature.

The monstrosity shambled in as if every move it made hurt. But the thing moved quickly enough when it saw Hobgoblin. "Formula!" it croaked in a horrible, thick voice. "Give back my formula!"

"A-A-Aron?" Elise Esterhazy faltered. She threw up both arms in front of her face as if to dispel the nightmare vision.

If someone knew what to look for, Spidey realized, *he might be able to recognize the remains of Aron Esterhazy in this creature.* From his recent superhuman handsomeness, the professor had turned into a cruel caricature of humanity.

The nose was still the same in the bloated face. But Esterhazy's white hair was completely gone. It was replaced by folds of loose flesh that looked like chicken skin over a monstrously misshapen skull.

The eyes were the right color. But instead of being cold, they were mad. The muscular body that Spider-Man remembered from only hours before was apparently still mutating right before their eyes.

"Formula!" the Esterhazy-monster screeched, plowing into Hobgoblin. A swipe of his bearish arm bowled over the villain.

Esterhazy pounced on the hypodermic, snatching it from Hobgoblin's hand. The experimental serum was still inside the needle's plastic tube.

"Aron, what happened to you?" wailed Elise Esterhazy.

"The formula," Esterhazy said painfully. "It keeps changing me. At first the changes were good, as I expected. The beneficial genes were strengthened."

"Physical perfection," Daredevil breathed.

"But the process didn't stop," the professor continued. "Other genes were bolstered. Recessive genes. Things began going wrong with my body." Esterhazy's lizard-hand clenched.

"Then it seemed my whole genetic record unspooled. There are so many things imprinted in our genes, a history of the progress of life. We still carry the codes for many of the lower forms, locked in each cell."

Elise Esterhazy's eyes went even wider with horror when she realized what her ex-husband was describing. The Kingpin's usually immobile face twitched. Hobgoblin gibbered while Daredevil frowned.

Everyone in the room stood immobile, as if some part of their brain had frozen as Esterhazy spoke. Spider-Man felt pity for his old professor—but the emotion was like an ice cube in a vast sea of horror.

"My genes have gone amok," Esterhazy continued in his awful, almost-human voice.

"I could see only one way—not to stop these tides of change, but to start the process all over again. To cycle back to the human."

The man-creature's mad eyes seemed to blaze. "I called David Borloff, told him to bring me certain ingredients. Then I reconstituted the formula, only to have it stolen. By *this*—"

Esterhazy's furred arm slammed out, the claws of his lizard-arm screeching along the Hobgoblin's armor. The sound was like fingernails on a blackboard.

Still, no one moved.

"No!" Esterhazy pulled himself back from his attack. "Can't waste time. Wasted too much already, trying to recreate the formula again—but I didn't have enough of the compounds. I found some of Fisk's searchers—made them tell me where they were supposed to take me . . ."

His voice trailed away in muttering to himself as he gazed at the hypodermic he clutched—his hoped-for salvation. His lizard-hand prepared to make the injection.

But when he went to plunge the needle in, Esterhazy seemed shocked to find fur on his arm. He tore at the remains of his coat and looked down on himself in dawning horror.

Since finding out where he had to go, Esterhazy had struggled on single-mindedly. Old

Doc Hazy had always been able to ignore the rest of the world while he worked. *No matter how much his body changed*, Spidey thought, *his mind stayed the same.*

And now that he stopped to focus again on his physical state, the professor discovered that he'd become a monstrosity. His reflection glittered up at him from a thousand shards of glass. "Too late!" he howled in a stricken voice.

Esterhazy tried to say more, but words failed him. A horrible noise came from deep in his chest. Black, stinking goo burst from his lips. It dribbled down his chin as he started to choke. The sticky stuff streamed across his body, matting down the fur and feathers.

The man was now beyond human help.

And the really horrible thing was that Esterhazy *knew* it. It was inescapable. He could see how every person in the room recoiled from him.

Aron Esterhazy looked down at the hypodermic he still clutched. Then he did the last thing he could as a human being. He tore the plunger out of the barrel of the injection device. Then he threw the opened needle out into the night through one of the empty solarium windows.

His life's work, the cruelly seductive formula for perfection, would die with him.

The effort was too much. Esterhazy over balanced and fell to the floor. His bod seemed to shrink, as if it were eating itsel from within. The pitiful creature jerked an slithered along the floor, leaving a slimy tra of protoplasm behind.

Then, at last, the thing that had been Aro Esterhazy lay still.

CHAPTER

—11—

The wrecked solarium was silent, except for Elise Esterhazy's gentle weeping. "Perfection was always Aron's obsession—something he craved," she said at last. "'Good nough' was never good enough for him."

She sobbed. "That attitude broke up our marriage. And now it's killed him."

Strangely enough, the sound of the other woman's crying seemed to bring Vanessa Fisk out of her daze. She hurried over to Elise Esterhazy, wordlessly trying to comfort her.

A new buzz of warning jangled in Spider-Man's brain. He turned to the most likely source of danger, his old enemy—the Kingpin. I can think of some other people who were esponsible," he said, glaring at the crime oss. "*Heavily* responsible."

The Kingpin snorted, his eyes growing nar row. After all that had happened, his tempe was on a hair trigger. Spidey knew that if he pressed a little more, this fight could go into round two. Right now, he felt it might be worth it.

Daredevil stepped between the two, saying "This is not the time—"

But the explosion that Spider-Man wa tensed for came from the other side of the room, from the Hobgoblin.

He had watched helplessly as the sole sam ple of the perfection formula was destroyed His obsession—to find the secret weapon that would let him destroy Spider-Man—had been denied yet again. Now, at the very least, he would have some revenge.

"You!" Hobgoblin howled, thrusting a fu rious finger at Spider-Man. "This is all you fault!"

Spidey turned from the Kingpin. "What' *your* problem, Hobbsy?" he asked. "You ge punched in the head once too often?"

"More likely, he's trying to arrange a dis traction so he can escape," the Kingpi growled.

Daredevil tried to appeal to reason. "Hob goblin, you saw what happened to Dr. Ester hazy. No one could have foreseen—"

"It's the insect, blast him! *He* did it!" Hob

goblin was lost in a world of his own. Rage seemed to turbo-charge his muscles. He rammed into Spider-Man, trying to strangle the surprised hero.

The kamikaze attack caught Spider-Man flat-footed. In fact, it caught *everyone* in the room off guard.

Hands like steel clamps clawed at Spidey's throat. The force of Hobgoblin's charge sent the two of them tumbling across the floor, until . . .

There was no longer any floor beneath their feet. They had tumbled right through the gap where one of the solarium's glass walls had been!

Hobgoblin didn't relax his death-grip even as they plummeted downward. *Great,* Spider-Man thought as he struggled to breathe. *I need one hand to get us to safety. That leaves only one hand to keep him from breaking my neck. But if I use both hands to pry away this stranglehold, we'll both fall and break our necks!*

He had to give it a try. Sticking out his left hand, he triggered his web-shooter. Nothing happened.

I never had time to reload after webbing up the jet-glider!

Struggling for breath, Spidey twisted around to get a shot off with his other hand.

A stream of webbing jetted out into the solarium's open wall and caught at the ceiling. Even as they jarred to a sudden stop, Spider-Man was using their new lifeline to swing his feet against the building's outer wall. They hit, held, and then he broke Hobgoblin's hold.

Just in time, Spidey thought. His lungs were burning for air, and the world had taken on a reddish hue.

"Look, genius," he gasped hoarsely, gripping the villain's wrists. "You can stop this nonsense, or you can try a forty-floor swan dive—without a jet-glider."

The Hobgoblin snarled, but remained quiet as Spider-Man went to web his wrists together. The hero's last web-cartridge sputtered— empty.

"Looks like the two of us almost did take that swan dive," Spidey said. He slowly crawled back up the wall, dragging his enemy along.

Hobgoblin continued to hold on tight until they reached the solarium. But no sooner did he have a floor under his feet than he lashed out at Spidey again.

Spider-Man dodged a vicious kick that would have sent him flying out the wrecked window again. "Now why did I expect that?" he said.

But Hobgoblin's attack was no joke. Even with his spider-powers, the hero wouldn't have survived that fall. Snarling, Hobgoblin went to aim his blasters, prepared to blow his enemy out the window. Then he squawked as a muscular arm closed around his neck and a knee landed in his spine.

"Enough!" Daredevil shouted, yanking the villain back.

Hobgoblin fought desperately to break free. He hurled himself in the direction Daredevil was pulling. Both men sprawled on the floor. Hobgoblin wormed his way out of Daredevil's slackened grip. But in a second Spider-Man was joining in, slapping fresh packs of web-fluid into his shooters.

The still-crazed villain leaped to his feet—just in time to ram into Spidey's right fist. Even as Hobgoblin went down, stunned, webbing gushed from Spider-Man's left-hand shooter. Sticky strands glued Hobgoblin's feet together—and onto the floor.

Daredevil grabbed the super-villain's wrists and heaved. In a second, Hobgoblin's arms were webbed together and glued down, too.

Spider-Man turned to the Kingpin, who had merely stood by, protecting the two women throughout the battle. Spidey massaged his throat, wondering if the Hobgoblin's hand had left bruises. "It was good of you to help, Fisk," he said sarcastically.

The Kingpin had returned to his usual, imperturbable self. "I've repaired the intercom," he said. "Assistance should be arriving shortly. There'll be medical aid for the doctor—and for my wife."

He turned to Elise Esterhazy. "My people will also do what they can for my guest here. I'm very sorry for your loss, Mrs. Esterhazy. The professor was a brilliant man. We'll arrange an escort to your home, and assist with the funeral arrangements."

Spidey noticed that Aron Esterhazy's body had been covered with a rug.

"Perhaps cremation," the Kingpin suggested.

"What about laughing boy over here?" Spider-Man demanded, jerking a thumb at Hobgoblin.

"He can stay as he is for the time being," the Kingpin replied.

"Right. I'm sure you'd like that—the guy who attacked you, all tied up. What are you going to do, try some batting practice with your cane? Or maybe you can have your boys toss him out the window."

The Kingpin merely gave him a glance of disdain. "I won't even discuss such suggestions. Besides, there's a much simpler way to achieve a most satisfying vengeance."

"Oh, really?" Spidey said.

"What do you intend to do?" Daredevil asked.

"I'll dial three numbers: 9-1-1. For someone like that—" the Kingpin's eyes took in the helpless Hobgoblin "—what could be more humiliating than to be taken by the police? A series of serious and embarrassing charges will be made."

"Attempted murder," said Spider-Man, still rubbing the bruises on his throat.

"Creating a public nuisance," was Daredevil's suggestion.

"There is always breaking and entering," the Kingpin added as he turned to confront the super heroes. "Although those charges could be applied just as well to you two."

"Yeah—same old Kingpin," Spider-Man said indignantly. "A 'legitimate businessman' who sends strong-arms after a respected professor. You kidnap his wife. An army of your *goons* chases him—not to mention the masked maniac over there. Then you steal his formula. And then you start making noises about breaking and entering! You ought to be *glad* we came in here right when we did. Considering what could have happened to your wife—"

Spider-Man looked at the distorted form under the rug. Then he gave the Kingpin a bitter glare. "But don't say *thank you* or anything."

"Spare me your self-righteous nonsense, little man," the Kingpin replied. "You don't like what I do—you've decided I'm a bad man. But, oddly enough, it's the good men of this world who are the greatest help to me, and are my best . . . resources."

Spidey was about to give him a furious answer when the Kingpin held up his hand. "I suppose you'd call Aron Esterhazy a *good man*. But he was happy to use my money for his research."

"He didn't know where it came from," Spidey cried.

"He didn't *care*," the Kingpin shot back. "And as long as such good men let themselves be used—there will be people like me. You yourself have proven to be useful," the crime boss said, nodding toward the webbed-up Hobgoblin.

"And you're ever so grateful," Daredevil said in a mocking voice.

The huge man looked down at them, his eyes expressionless. "You're still alive, aren't you?" he asked softly.

"Let's get out of here, Daredevil," Spider-Man said. "There's no talking to this guy. He just makes me want to break something."

Spidey glanced around the wrecked room. "And there's nothing left to break."

Two super heroes stood on the roof of the skyscraping office tower. With the arrival of the police and emergency crews, they had decided to leave the way they had come. Neither of them cared to spend the better part of the next day explaining to the authorities what had happened.

"Two days without sleep, tangling with punks, mad scientists, and the Hobgoblin," Spider-Man said. "And what do I have to show for it? Bruises all around my neck—and the knowledge that we've done a favor for the Kingpin. And in response, he has graciously decided that he won't kill us. I guess that's why the automatic roof defenses are off."

"Either that, or the circuits are just burned out." Daredevil said with a tired laugh.

"So what are you going to do?" Spidey asked.

Daredevil shrugged. "Climb my way down this big box, avoid the police, then head back to Hell's Kitchen."

"To sleep?"

The red-clad super hero shook his head, rubbing a slightly stubbled chin. "Not yet. I want to make sure the Kingpin's army has been pulled out. The search should have been called off by now. But as we saw downstairs, things are a little disorganized in the Kingpin's headquarters. And you?"

Spider-Man jerked up straight, jolted by a sudden thought. "Oh, man! I've got to get out to Forest Hills!"

"Trouble with your aunt?" Daredevil asked.

Spidey nodded. "She's not feeling well. And when you get to be her age . . ." He was silent for a second. "It's too bad Dr. Esterhazy's formula didn't work out. It could have done a lot of good for a lot of sick people."

"*Perfection*," Daredevil said in an odd tone of voice. "I guess it's too much to hope for— at least, for us plain humans."

"That's not like you, DD," Spider-Man said. "You sound like the guys in the old horror movies." He deepened his voice. 'There are some doors that shouldn't be opened.' "

The corners of Daredevil's mouth turned up slightly, but he didn't laugh. "Maybe they were right."

And maybe, Spidey suddenly realized, *you shouldn't offer hope to a blind man.*

He watched in silence as Daredevil went to the back edge of the roof, slipped over, and began the long climb down.

Spider-Man's journey led in the opposite direction. He checked his web-shooters, walked to the eastern side of the building, and prepared to set off for Queens. "Web-line express," he muttered.

Thwip! He shot a line of webbing to the top of the roof's tower and vaulted off. Then he shot a new line to a lower building nearby. As he swung away, Spidey glanced back at the box the Kingpin had built around himself.

He found himself looking down into the wrecked solarium. A pair of nurses were leading Vanessa Fisk away. A throng of detectives, uniformed officers and doctors filled the destroyed solarium. The Kingpin stood with his back to them, his head down. As Spidey watched, the big man took a few small objects out of his pocket. They sparkled, like crystal. He seemed to be trying to fit them together. *Looks like something else of great value was lost during the fight*, Spider-Man thought.

The Kingpin himself looked at though he had been broken by the events of the evening.

Maybe my life isn't perfect, Spidey thought. *But it's better than what some people have.*

He shook his head as though to clear it, and swung east—toward Forest Hills, Aunt May, and Mary Jane.

YOU ARE SPIDER-MAN
VERSUS
THE SINISTER SIX

You are Peter Parker, the Amazing Spider-Man. You are fighting hidden enemies, and your trusted spider-sense seems to have gone crazy. Mary Jane is in danger. Innocent lives are threatened. You must make the correct decisions in the heat of battle, or lives will be lost. But can you defeat Mysterio, the Chameleon, the Hobgoblin, the Shocker, the Vulture . . . and Doctor Octopus . . . before the bomb that they've planted kills hundreds of people?

The decisions are yours to make, because

YOU ARE SPIDER-MAN!

At Bookstores Everywhere, August 1996.

IRON MAN SUPER THRILLER:
STEEL TERROR

Iron Man and his fellow Avengers are presented with their greatest challenge yet: how to stop the invincible super-robot Ultron from accomplishing his goal. Simply put, Ultron is ready and able to destroy the human race—wipe it off the planet completely and for all time. From New York City to the frozen wastes of Antarctica, Iron Man must race the clock to find Ultron, defeat his robotic monsters, and save the rest of the Avengers from death by fire and ice.

BE THERE OR BE FRIED!

At Bookstores Everywhere, October 1996

Introducing an all-new series!

SPIDER-MAN®

Spider-Man Super Thriller #1
Midnight Justice by Martin Delrio
56851-5/$4.99

Spider-Man Super Thriller #2
Deadly Cure by Bill McCay
00320-8/$4.99

And for younger readers
Spider-Man: You Are Spider-Man #1
by Richie Chevat
00319-4/$3.99

Available from Pocket Books